PEGGY GOODY

and the

MAGIC TRIANGLE

Peggy Goody
and the
Magic Triangle

Charles S. Hudson

Trafford rev. 10/16/2012

 www.trafford.com

North America & international
toll-free: 1 888 232 4444 (USA & Canada)
phone: 250 383 6864 ♦ fax: 812 355 4082

CONTENTS

Chapter 1

THE FAIRY BLUEBELL

The sun rose lazily and the villagers of Little Thatch woke to a beautiful morning. The sky was blue and clear, and the sound of birds singing their early morning songs could be heard, welcoming a new day. It was Sunday and Rose Goody and her twelve-year-old daughter Peggy were preparing breakfast. Sunday was always special to them because it was the one day they could sit down together and not have to rush.

Rose ran her own little laundry business serving the village, and that meant for six days of the week it was six early morning starts. But Sunday was their day, a special day and time to take it easy, catch up, and enjoy their girl talk. They talked about the past week and all the various things that had happened. Peggy talked about school, and the things that she had done with her best friend, Cindy, and Rose talked about the past week and the people she had seen. Then after about an hour of talking and laughing had passed, they started to clear away breakfast.

'Are you going over to see Cindy today?' Rose enquired.

'No mother, not today. She's visiting her aunt. I thought I could go down to the meadow and pick some bluebells to put on the kitchen table.' Rose nodded in agreement, and agreed they would look very nice. 'But I want you to stay clear of the forest. You know how dangerous it can be. All sorts of bad things go on inside there, and it's no place for a young girl to go wandering off by herself.' Peggy promised her mother she would stay in the meadow and keep away from the forest, and when they had finished clearing away, she picked up her flower basket and off she went.

She was singing as she walked along in the meadow, and was just about to start picking her flowers when in the distance she saw a large patch of bluebells that were down by the forest. 'I bet they are the best in the meadow,' she thought, and started to walk over to them. But as she went near, the bluebells seemed to move away, as if by magic, taking her closer and closer to the forest. When she finally reached them, she could see they were the most beautiful big bluebells and thought how much her mother would love them. Just as she was about to start picking, she thought she could hear a voice calling for help, coming from inside the forest. Without thinking she started to walk in the direction of the sound, going deeper and deeper through the trees, until she could hear the voice quite clearly. Peggy looked around but could not see anyone, and then, without any warning, the forest seemed to get darker, and she started to feel cold. The trees seemed to close in around her, and she had a terrible feeling of being watched.

Her mother had warned her not to go into the forest, and just because a voice had called for help she had abandoned all caution and plunged in without a second thought. 'What if it was a trap? she thought. The forest was known to be enchanted and several travellers had vanished after entering, never to be seen again. She looked up, and the sky had turned an angry purple colour, and Peggy sensed she was not alone. She turned and peered into the darkness and her blood ran cold.

Staring back at her were creatures with bright red eyes. She let out a piercing scream and dropped to her knees. Rain drops had started to fall through the trees and she felt terrified. Peggy looked all around but there was no obvious path out and she thought, 'What am I going to do?' There was a rustling noise in the trees just behind her, and when she turned around to look at what had made the noise she was face to face with a red hairy creature. She stared at it unable to move, frozen with fear.

Then suddenly a voice called out, 'Up here.' Peggy looked and to her surprise, at the top of the tree, was a beautiful blue fairy. 'Don't be afraid,' she said. 'The creatures are Demodoms. They will not harm you while I am here. They are waiting, hoping I will fall asleep so they can climb up and capture me. I've been trapped up here for over an hour, said the fairy, and I have broken one of my wings. Will you help me?'

Peggy had not climbed trees before, but she was not afraid. The tree was very tall, and it would take all her will power to reach the fairy; but without any hesitation she started to climb up the trunk. It was slippery and the rain was getting heavy, so she had to be careful and move slowly. But after a lot of slipping and sliding she reached the first big branch, and scrambled onto it to rest, but she could see she still had a long way to go. Several of the Demodoms had climbed up into the trees circling her, sitting quietly, not moving, they just stared at her with their big red eyes. Then, after a few minutes, she stood and began to climb again, branch by branch. It was so difficult because her feet kept slipping off the smaller branches, but she clung on for dear life. The Demodoms were matching her every move, and they all went higher and higher together. Slowly Peggy was getting closer to the fairy, but she was getting tired and her arms and legs were hurting. She kept telling herself not to look down or at the Demodoms and to keep moving.

At last, she was level with the fairy. 'Can you move at all?' Peggy asked the fairy. The fairy said not very much. 'I think I have broken my leg as well as my wing.' Peggy sat on a branch. She was so tired now she could hardly move. She had used up all her strength climbing the tree and now she had to rest and think of a way to get back down while carrying the fairy.

Peggy looked at the fairy and asked her who the Demodoms were? The fairy said the Demodoms were part monkey and part Gnome, and their leader Demodus was a giant Gnome. He was an outcast from Greco City in the land of the Gnomes. About one thousand years ago he had been caught trying to steal gold from the Rainbow Bank that was owned by the Leprechauns; in the fight that took place while they were trying to defend the bank and capture him, Demodus had killed three Leprechauns.

He would have gotten away with it, had not the Golden Fairy Queen been watching him in the pool of wisdom. She had cast a spell over him and rendered him motionless, and then she had handed him over to Igor the King of the Gnomes.

Igor had put Demodus on trial, and he was found guilty of murder. They stripped him of his wealth and possessions, and banished him from Greco, and he was sent into exile, in the wilderness of the North Pole.

About two hundred years ago he had turned up here in the forest with his band of Demodoms, and ever since then he has vowed to get his revenge on Igor and the fairy world. There are stories of travellers who had lost their way in the forest and wandered until they had fallen asleep exhausted. The Demodoms had found them and taken them back to Demodus. Once there, he would torture them and gain all their knowledge to add to his own, and each time he did it he became more powerful, and more travellers disappeared, never to be seen again.

The fairy could see how tired Peggy was and reached out to her. 'Take my hand,' she said, and as they touched a tingling sensation ran through Peggy's body from head to toe. After a few moments the fairy removed her hand and Peggy felt her strength return. 'Don't be afraid,' said the fairy, 'It is just a little bit of fairy magic. I have given you some of my energy. It will do you no harm, and as soon as I return to the ground and touch Mother Earth all my energy will return.' Peggy now knew that somehow she had to get the fairy onto her back and quickly carry her down.

When the fairy had crashed into the tree, she had broken the branch where she was lying, and it looked as if at any moment it could break and send the fairy plummeting down, and she knew she must act quickly. Carefully she put her feet onto separate branches to give her a solid platform, and then reached over to the fairy and held her tightly underneath her arms. Peggy pulled the fairy towards her with all the strength she could muster, and just as she lifted her, the branch the fairy had been lying on snapped off and hurtled to the ground. Peggy screamed and almost slipped, but she managed to get the fairy onto her back, where she clung on with both hands around Peggy's neck.

Her one wing was hanging down by her side and her leg was broken, and the poor fairy was in a lot of pain. Peggy was as careful as she could be, when suddenly there was a cracking sound and the branch Peggy had just stepped onto snapped. They were falling towards the ground. Peggy let go of the fairy with one hand and by some miracle managed to hook her arm over a branch of the tree as it came up to meet her. They dangled there for a while swinging backwards and forwards on the branch. Peggy was soaking wet and she could feel her grip slipping. She was desperately searching for something to put her feet on, when suddenly her foot brushed against something, and with her last ounce of energy she made a big swing and managed to stand on a branch lower down the tree. She had hurt her arm in the fall and it took a massive effort to carry on, but she was never going to give in. There was a sudden flash of lightning and an ear splitting clap of thunder, Peggy screamed and almost let go of the tree it frightened her so much, but she held on and slowly managed to climb down to the ground, where she lay exhausted. They both lay together on the ground, and once again the fairy reached out and touched Peggy on the shoulder and the same tingling feeling went through her body. After a few minutes the fairy removed her hand, and Peggy could feel her strength coming back. There were Demodoms standing all around them circling in a menacing silence. 'Don't be afraid,' said the fairy. She took out her wand and pointed it at one of the Demodoms. 'Boltus!' she cried, and a bolt of bright light shot out and hit him. He squealed and started to run away followed closely by the other Demodoms. 'They will leave us alone now,' said the fairy. 'Now that they know I can use my magic against them, and they can see that I have regained my strength and can defend myself.'

The fairy took Peggy by the hand. 'I am so sorry for all the trouble I have caused you, and for using my magic to entice you to come into the forest, but I had no choice. If the Demodoms had taken me prisoner it would have been disastrous for the fairy world. I have got you to do all of this for me and I don't even know your name.' 'It's Peggy. Peggy Goody. I live with my mother in Little Thatch Village.'

'My name is Bluebell,' said the fairy, 'and I gather information for the Silver Fairy. The Silver Fairy looks after all of the fairies in the land for the Golden Fairy, who is our Queen, and she lives in the Golden Fairy Cave in Ireland. If you can carry me back home to the Silver Cave, you will meet the Silver Fairy, and I am sure she will be very happy to see you, and grateful that you have helped me, and prevented me from falling into the clutches of the Demodoms.'

On the way to the Silver Cave Bluebell explained to Peggy that all of the fairies and the Fairy Kingdom where they lived were invisible to humans and all the creatures of the forest. When Peggy had picked up Bluebell and held her in her arms she had become invisible, too. Bluebell explained that she was hazing. It was a high speed vibration that the fairies could do to make them blend into the background wherever they were, thus rendering them invisible to the naked eye. And now because she was carrying Bluebell she had also become invisible and she would be able to see everything when she arrived at the Fairy Kingdom. Bluebell guided Peggy through the forest as they went along, with Peggy carrying Bluebell in her arms. It was very painful for her because she had hurt her arm much more than she had first thought when they had fallen through the tree.

When they arrived at the Fairy Kingdom, there were hundreds of fairies all buzzing around, pointing at Peggy and asking what had happened to Bluebell. 'A human here in the Fairy Kingdom? How was it possible?' Suddenly all the fairies fell silent. The Silver Fairy had come to see what all the noise was about. 'Good heavens,' she said when she saw Peggy. 'Bluebell, what have you done?' Then the Silver Fairy realised that Bluebell was seriously hurt. She looked at Peggy and said 'Please follow me,' and led Peggy to the Silver Cave. It was the most beautiful thing that Peggy had ever seen.

Bluebell explained how she had been flying through the forest and a branch had fallen from a tree and hit her, sending her crashing into another tree, where she had lain hurt and trapped. She told the Silver Fairy how she had been unable to haze and the Demodoms had spotted her lying there injured in the tree, and how they had been waiting for a chance to capture her and take her back to the mines and give her to Demodus. And how by pure chance she had heard Peggy singing in the meadow close to the forest, and had enticed her in, and called out for her help. She told the Silver Fairy the whole story of Peggy's climb up the tall tree, and her injury, and how brave and kind she had been. The Silver Fairy was very grateful to Peggy, and said it had taken a very brave girl to do all this, and to show her gratitude she would give her a Magic Gift. From this day on I will give you the magic power to stretch your legs to any length you want.

'Now, Peggy, stand before me,' and as Peggy stood there the Silver Fairy touched her on the shoulder with her magic wand. 'Now I want you to say "UP-UP" until you are as high as you wish to go, and then say "DOWN-DOWN" and you will return to your normal size.' Peggy was very excited and said 'UP-UP' and her legs began to get longer and longer until she had reached the top of the Silver Cave. Then she said 'DOWN-DOWN' until she was back to her normal size. 'Wow,' said Peggy, 'how amazing is that?' The Silver Fairy looked at Peggy and said, 'Peggy, this magic will only work if it is used for good purposes, and if you should ever abuse your magic in any way for personal gain, you will lose it. From now on there will be no more climbing about in trees for you, young lady. Now let me have a look at your arm where you hurt yourself.'

Peggy tried to lift it but it hurt too much. The Silver Fairy touched Peggy with her magic wand and the pain vanished. 'Thank you,' said Peggy. The Silver Fairy smiled at Peggy and said, 'It is I who should be thanking you, and I hope that we will meet again soon, some time in the near future. And now you must leave us. Bluebell will show you the way home. Good luck with all that you do and, Peggy, remember your magic must only be used for good purposes.'

Bluebell said, 'Follow me, Peggy,' and fluttered her wings. The Silver Fairy had healed her broken wing and leg and off she flew, guiding the way. As soon as they were back in the forest Bluebell asked Peggy to hold her hand so she could haze and they could walk through the forest without being seen by the Demodoms. Then she led her to the place where Peggy was going to pick her bluebells next to a great oak tree. Bluebell stared into Peggy's eyes and placed a non-remembrance spell on her. And, finally, she said, 'If you ever think you are in danger, I want you to say the words "BLUE FLASH HELP"; and I will come to you immediately. From now on the Silver Fairy has charged me to keep you safe, but you must remember to call me.' Then she said goodbye and, with a flash of blue light, disappeared. Peggy finished picking her bluebells and returned home, and could not remember where she had been, but she could remember the magic gift that she had been given by the Silver Fairy.

In a far corner of the forest the Demodoms had returned to the mine. Demodus was waiting for them. 'Well,' he roared, 'where is the fairy?' The largest of the Demodoms stepped forward and dropped to his knees. 'Forgive me, master,' he said, grovelling at his feet. 'We were almost ready to capture her, when suddenly a human appeared from out of nowhere. She climbed the tree and helped the fairy to escape, but before they disappeared I heard the human say that her name was Peggy Goody, and she lived in the village of Little Thatch. I also heard the fairy say that her name was Bluebell.'

'Bluebell!' screamed Demodus. 'She is the most magical fairy next to the Silver Fairy. You fool. Do you realise that we have lost the chance to learn more fairy magic than we could ever have dreamed of? And now we have a human enemy as well, this so called Peggy Goody!' He stormed off into his mine cursing out loud as he went.

Peggy sat down at the kitchen table that evening and told her mother she had had a lovely time picking bluebells, and in the morning she had a big surprise to show her, but she wanted to practise first before she could see it. Rose Goody thought whatever can she be talking about, but she didn't ask her what it was, because Peggy obviously wanted to give her a surprise in the morning. That night Peggy lay in bed thinking about Bluebell and the Silver Fairy. Tomorrow she would show her mother how her new magic worked, and as she fell asleep she wondered what new and exciting adventures lay ahead.

Chapter 2

THE POST OFFICE FIRE

Peggy was up early the next morning, and was busily practicing with her new magic legs. As soon as her mother was dressed Peggy called her to come outside to see her surprise: she was going to be the first person ever to see Peggy make her legs grow. 'Well now, Peggy, what's the big surprise?' her mother asked. 'Watch this,' said Peggy, and said out loud 'UP-UP' and in an instant she was level with the cottage roof. Then she said 'DOWN-DOWN' and was suddenly back down to normal. 'My goodness!' shouted Rose, almost falling backwards with surprise. 'How long have you been able to do that?' she asked. Peggy laughed and told her about Bluebell the fairy and the Silver Fairy making her legs magic, but she could not remember why or how. 'Well,' said Rose, 'if I hadn't seen it for myself I wouldn't have believed it. Has anyone else seen you do it?' 'No,' said Peggy, 'not yet. I wanted you to be the first one.'

That afternoon Peggy and her mother went into the village to do some food shopping, and went first to the butchers. 'Good afternoon,' said Bob the butcher, 'what can I get you ladies? I've got some lovely legs of lamb, fresh in from the farm.' Peggy looked at her mother and they both burst out laughing. 'What's funny about that?' asked Bob, frowning. 'Take no notice of us,' said Rose; 'it's just a private joke between us.' They bought some sausages and bacon and chatted to Bob for a few minutes before leaving.

The next stop was the green grocers. 'Good afternoon,' said Jack Sprout 'isn't it a lovely day?' But before they could answer him there was a loud shout of 'FIRE-FIRE' and everyone came running out of the shops to see where the noise was coming from—it was the Post Office. And as they all stood watching, they could hear the sound of the fire engine bells racing towards them. As soon as the fire engine arrived the firemen jumped out, pulling the hoses into place and within minutes they were spraying water onto the flames.

Suddenly there was a cry coming from one of the bedroom windows, and as they looked up, there was the figure of Billy, the young son of Mr and Mrs Stamp, who ran the post office. They were all pointing up at the bedroom window and shouting to the firemen. The firemen began to swing the extending ladder around to face the window when, suddenly, there was panic—the ladder was stuck, it just would not move. The smoke was getting worse and the fire was spreading, 'HELP ME,—HELP ME,' screamed Billy. Mr Stamp dashed toward the door of the post office, only to be met by a fireman barring his way. 'You can't go in there,' he said, 'It's far too dangerous.' 'But my son is in there!' shouted Mr Stamp. 'I know,' said the fireman, 'but we don't want to have to rescue two of you, so please leave it to us, and please move back.' Mr Stamp reluctantly agreed and went back to where his wife was standing. 'They won't let me go in,' he said, and put his arm around his wife, pulling her close.

The ladder still would not release and the firemen were getting desperate. Peggy realised what was happening and dashed past the firemen, who were frantically trying to free the ladder. She stood under the bedroom window, hidden from view. 'UP-UP,' she shouted, and in a second she was level with Billy. But as she was about to call to him, a thick cloud of black smoke covered her and she could not breathe, and was choking. 'DOWN—DOWN,' she cried, and came back down to the ground, coughing, and her eyes watering.

Billy was screaming and tears were running down his face. He could barely breathe and was almost ready to collapse. 'BLUE FLASH HELP!' screamed Peggy out loud, and in a second Bluebell was by her side. 'It's little Billy Stamp, he's trapped up in his bedroom, but when I got up close to him a thick black cloud of smoke covered me and I couldn't breathe.' 'It's the Fire Imp,' said Bluebell. 'They will try to stop you from saving Billy. They want to steal his soul and take it back to the Fire Pit and their master Furnusabal. Peggy, you have got to go back up there now, and don't worry, I will help you; we haven't a second to spare!'

'UP-UP,' shouted Peggy, and as she drew level with Billy's bedroom window a massive gust of wind blew the smoke away. As Peggy looked up she could see hundreds of little black figures dancing on the roof. They looked evil and were pointing at her with long sharp claw-like fingers. 'Put your arms around my neck, Billy,' she shouted, 'and hold on tight.' Billy jumped into Peggy's arms and she shouted 'DOWN-DOWN' and as soon as they were back on the ground they ran from the fire.

Billy and Peggy lay on the ground gasping for breath. A fireman came rushing up with two oxygen masks. 'Put this on and take some deep breaths,' he said to Peggy. 'I'll take care of the little one.' He kneeled down and placed a mask over Billy's face. Bluebell had made sure they were both safe, and then disappeared. Mr and Mrs Stamp came running over and picked up Billy and began to hug him. He was coughing and crying, and covered in black grime from the fire. 'Thank God you're safe. We thought we'd lost you!' sobbed Mrs Stamp. They both turned to Peggy and said 'We don't know how you did it, Peggy, but thank you so much for saving our Billy.'

Everyone stood still and looked at Peggy in amazement. They could not believe what had just happened. Was it possible Peggy had stretched her legs long enough to reach the bedroom window? The Chief Fireman came over to Peggy and put his arm around her and said, 'You are the bravest person I ever met in all of my time in the service, and I thank you for what you did today, and that goes for all of us at the station.' Suddenly the crowd began to shout 'Peggy Goody—Peggy Goody!' and one voice in the crowd shouted 'It should be Leggy Peggy!' and the crowd began to laugh and shout 'Leggy Peggy!' It was a nickname that would stay with her for a long time.

Deep in the forest there was another side to the story. The Fire Imps had arrived back at the Fire Pit, in the middle of a large clearing. Their Master, Furnusabal, was waiting for them. 'Where is Billy Stamp's soul?' he demanded. The leader of the Fire Imp, Yellow Flame, stepped forward, bowing his head. 'Master, we were just about ready to take it when a young girl appeared and snatched him from our very grasp, and because of her we haven't got it.' 'Fire and Brimstone!' roared Furnusabal.

'You will pay for this! Into the pit all of you and you can stay in there for ten days and bake. A young girl, I don't believe it. With all the trouble that I have with those interfering fairies, it looks like they have joined forces with a human. Damnation!' he roared, and kicked the last few Fire Imps into the Fire Pit with his big clawed foot.

Rose Goody could see that Peggy had used up all her energy in the rescue and took her straight home. As soon as they were inside she ran a hot bath and Peggy lay there soaking, and afterward, when she came downstairs, there was a hot mug of chocolate and a piece of apple pie waiting for her. That night Peggy lay in bed awake thinking about Billy Stamp and how close he had come to losing his soul to the wicked Fire Imps. Then her mind drifted to Bluebell. She had been there for her the instant she had called; it was to be the start of a strong and true friendship that would last forever and would see them through many adventures. She dropped off into a deep sleep.

Two days later a van pulled up outside Peggy's house, and a man got out and knocked on the door. Rose opened the door and said in a surprised voice, 'Mr Sparks, whatever brings you down here?' Mr Sparks owned the electrical goods shop in the village. 'I've brought your new washing machine,' he said, 'and I've come to fix it up for you today.' Rose looked shocked and said there must be some mistake. 'I haven't ordered a washing machine, I could certainly use one, but I can't run to it yet. It's only four months since you fitted the last one for me.'

'You don't have to pay for it,' explained Mr Sparks, 'It's a gift from the village. They put together a collection because of the brave thing that your Peggy did, with her risking her own safety to save little Billy Stamp. We all know how hard you work in the laundry, and we thought this machine would lighten your burden.'

'I don't know what to say,' said Rose, shaking her head. 'Peggy would never expect to gain from helping someone.'

'It was a little bit more than helping Billy,' said Mr Sparks, 'Peggy saved his life and we all know it.' 'Thank you,' said Rose, 'Oh, thank you, and I will put it to good use, I can promise you that.' She sounded choked and gave Mr Sparks a hug.

'Now don't you get upsetting yourself,' said Mr Spark's, 'or you'll start me off. Right, let's get to work.' When Mr Sparks had finished installing the washing machine he tested it to make sure everything was in good working order. 'Come and have a look, Mrs Goody. I want to show you how it works.' Rose already had two machines for her laundry business—one was an old thing on its last legs, and the other was new, but this one had everything and took a much bigger load. She was so excited her hands were shaking. 'Just look at me, Mr Sparks,' she said, holding up her hands. 'There's no need to be nervous with this machine,' he said, 'it looks after itself.' Rose had two practice runs and was happy she could manage on her own. 'Now, Mr Sparks,' said Rose, 'is there anything that I can do for you?' 'A cup of tea would be nice,' said Mr Sparks, and they both started to laugh. Rose sat with Mr Sparks, sipping her tea and chatting. What a wonderful day she was having, and what a big surprise Peggy would have when she came home from school. 'I'm off now,' said Mr Sparks, 'got a busy day ahead. Oh, and before I go, there are two big boxes of washing powder by the side of the machine! Must dash!' and off he went.

Chapter 3

THE LITTLE TABBY CAT

Demodus was sitting at the entrance of his mine, still annoyed with his Demodoms for losing the fairy Bluebell. He was expecting a visitor at any moment: Furnusabal, Master of the Fire Imps. They worked together for mutual gain. Demodus helped Furnusabal by tunnelling to the places where he wanted to set his fires, so he could kill people and capture their souls, and in return Furnusabal sent heat through a series of shafts that the Demodoms had carved out of the rock and earth, to keep the mines warm all year round.

'Greetings, friend!' roared Furnusabal, as he caught sight of Demodus. Demodus roared back, 'Welcome, my friend!' and held out his hand. 'Come and sit with me and tell me what you've been up to.' Furnusabal sat down and began telling him the story of the fire at the post office in Little Thatch Village. 'We had a boy trapped in his bedroom and we were all ready to steal his soul, when a young girl shot up from the ground and snatched him from our grasp, and I'm sure that she possesses fairy magic because the thick smoke we created was suddenly blown away by a powerful gust of wind.'

'That is very interesting,' said Demodus. 'Did she have a name?' 'Peggy Goody, the crowd called her Peggy Goody.' 'I might have guessed,' said Demodus, and he told Furnusabal about the fairy that was trapped in the tree and that the same girl had rescued her right from under the noses of his Demodoms. They had been within minutes of capturing her until that nosey Peggy Goody appeared from nowhere. 'Who is she, anyway?' asked Furnusabal.

'I don't know, but I think it confirms my suspicions that she has fairy magic. We need to lay a trap and capture her before she wrecks any more of our plans.'

They talked and schemed together until they both agreed on a trap they would set to capture Peggy. It would be simple, and something she would fall into without thinking it was dangerous. Furnusabal had an idea that they may be able to lure Peggy Goody down to the old mill, trap her inside, get the Fire Imps to set fire to it, and maybe capture her soul at the same time. Demodus sat there thinking. 'It is not a bad plan,' he said, 'but I think it would draw to much attention to us. But it has given me an idea. If I remember correctly, there's a dried up well outside the old mill, and it's about ten metres deep. If, as you suggest, we could somehow get Peggy Goody to go down to the mill say, with a friend to have a picnic, then we could put something into the well to make her want to go down. It's about two miles from here to the bottom of the well, so it wouldn't take me long to cut a tunnel leading to there.'

It is, of course, well known that gnomes are master tunnel diggers. With powerful arms and hard sharp claws they can protrude from the back of their fingers, and when they want to dig a tunnel the gnome stretches his arms above his head with his claws facing the way he wants to go. Then he spins his body round at an enormous speed cutting through the ground as if it were made of butter. This was the only piece of gnome magic that Igor had allowed Demodus to keep when he was sent into exile.

Demodus looked over to Furnusabal. 'Do you still possess your magic power of suggestion?' 'Yes,' said Furnusabal, 'why?'

'We need to plant a thought into the mind of Peggy Goody's friend. It's Friday today so we have plenty of time, in fact it could be done on her way home from school. Could you manage to put a thought into her mind, and make her think she would like to have a picnic with Peggy on Sunday at the old mill by the river?'

'No trouble at all,' said Furnusabal, 'What's the plan?'

'Well, if we can get them both down by the well, I will arrange for someone's pet cat to be trapped down there, and nosey Peggy Goody will not be able to resist going down to rescue it. She will have no idea that some of my Demodoms will be down there waiting for her. They will bind her legs together and drag her off, back to the mine. Then when we get her back to the mine, we can force her to tell us where the fairy camp is, and we can tunnel underneath it, and then, LOOK OUT FAIRIES!' They both screamed out loud in devilish laughter. 'Let's get started right away,' said Furnusabal, stamping his big ugly clawed feet and sending up clouds of dust.

And almost as they had planned, Peggy called in on her best friend, Cindy, who lived in Little Thatch. They were in the same class at school and worked and played together almost every day.

It was Sunday and they had decided to have a picnic by the river by the old flour mill. It wasn't very far away, just at the end of the village. Cindy's mother had prepared a bag of goodies, with a bottle of lemonade, a large packet of potato crisps, two apples and two bananas, what a feast they were going to have. They took it in turns to carry the bag, because it was quite heavy. When they arrived at the spot they chose for their picnic they laid the bag on the ground and started to play ball. They soon were hot and thirsty and decided to stop and have a drink of lemonade, and as they sat there quietly drinking, a boy from the village, Charlie Lacey, who lived in the shoe shop, came up to them. 'Have you seen a tabby cat wandering around here?' he asked. 'No,' said the girls, 'but we haven't been here very long. Would you like us to help you look for him?' asked Cindy. 'Yes, please,' said Charlie. 'I call him Tiger, because he has four black stripes on his back. He's been missing since breakfast this morning.' Peggy said, 'If I go and look for him along the river bank, then you can both look for him around by the mill' they agreed the plan and went off in different directions.

Peggy had walked about a quarter of a mile along the river bank, when she thought she could hear something in the rushes. She stopped and went closer to the river to look at what was making the noise, and as she got closer a duck suddenly swam out into the river with seven ducklings following. Peggy gave a sigh of relief. And then, just as she was about to carry on along the bank, she heard Cindy calling her, so she turned and started to walk back. When Cindy caught up to her she said, 'We think we found Tiger. We can hear a cry coming from down in the bottom of the dried up well next to the mill.' The girls hurried back and when they got there, Charlie was calling 'Tiger' down into the well and, as they listened, a faint 'MEEE-OWWW' rose from below. 'Let's look to see if we can find a rope in the mill,' suggested Charlie, and they started to search, but after ten minutes had to give up. 'What are we going to do now?' Cindy cried. 'I will have to go back to the village and get the firemen to bring a ladder,' said Charlie.

But Peggy had an idea. 'If you both hold my arms I can dangle my legs down the well and make them grow until they touch the bottom. Then I can go down to my normal size pick up Tiger and make my legs grow again and bring him up. I can then sit on the side of the well and go back to normal size again!' Charlie said, it's a good idea, but won't it be dangerous? What if you get stuck down there with Tiger?' Peggy said 'I can go down slowly and I can feel if there is anything in the way with my feet.'

So Peggy got up onto the well and Cindy and Charlie held her arms as she dangled her legs into the depths below. 'UP-UP,' she said, and her legs went down to the bottom of the well. 'It feels safe enough,' she said. 'You can let me go.' Then, as they released her arms she said 'DOWN-DOWN' and down she went to the bottom. Peggy stood in the dark and could hear Tiger crying. Then she felt him rubbing himself up against her leg. 'Come on, Tiger,' she said, and picked him up. 'I think you have had enough of this place.' But before she could say another word a voice shouted 'Got you!' and a powerful pair of hands grabbed her. Peggy could feel a rope being tied around her legs and she was being dragged down the dark tunnel that had been dug from the mine in the forest. It was a trap! Peggy held Tiger close to her and shouted 'Blue Flash Help!' Suddenly there was a loud bang and a flash of blue light. The Demodom gave out a scream and let go of Peggy's legs, and ran back up the tunnel towards the forest. Bluebell helped Peggy back to the bottom of the well. 'I'm afraid you have made some enemies in the creature world,' she said.

'Earlier today the Demodoms stole Tiger and put him down into the well. They knew that when Charlie Lacey asked if you had seen him, you would help look, and it would lead you down into the well where they were waiting to capture you. I couldn't interfere until you called for me. I don't think they will try again, but be on your guard just in case. Now go back up to your friends. They won't know what has happened down here.' And with a flash of blue light she disappeared. Peggy said 'UP-UP' and suddenly they were back into the daylight. Peggy passed Tiger over to Charlie, then sat on the top of the well and said 'DOWN-DOWN' and her legs went back to normal.

When they were walking away from the well Charlie began crying with joy, 'I thought I would never see you again,' he said to Tiger. 'Thank you, Peggy, or should I say, "Leggy Peggy"' and they all burst out laughing. 'If only they knew what had just happened down in the well I don't think they would be laughing,' thought Peggy. Charlie hadn't really lost Tiger, he had been stolen, but he would never know. He joined the girls and they all had a lovely picnic. 'I can't wait till I get home and tell everybody what happened today,' said Charlie. Peggy just smiled. They packed away the empty bottle and scraps of fruit into the bag. Peggy's mother always said, 'Don't leave your rubbish for other people to clear up,' and when they were finished they walked back toward the village talking and laughing, and then went their separate ways.

On the way home Peggy wondered what would happen if her mother ever discovered what had happened. She knew she could never tell her and it would have to remain a secret between her and Bluebell. Peggy lay in bed that night thinking about the events of the past few weeks. She had seen the Demodoms and the Fire Imps, but she had not seen their masters. But if she only knew what they looked like, she wouldn't have wanted to.

The Demodom scampered along the tunnel, his one leg was dragging; he was in agony, because Bluebell had hit him with a powerful sting spark. When he got to the other end of the tunnel he staggered out into the daylight. He saw another Demodom standing close by. 'Bring me some water!' he screamed, and the Demodom was so startled he fell over backwards, got up, and ran towards the well. In no time he was back with a bucket of water. The Demodom lifted the bucket up to his wide ugly mouth and in three massive gulps drank it all.

Demodus had been waiting by the tunnel for his return. 'Great Balls of Fire!' he roared when he saw the Demodom. 'What's happened?' he demanded. 'Peggy Goody and that dammed fairy, that's what happened,' said the Demodom, holding his leg in pain. 'Everything went exactly as you had planned it. She came down to the bottom of the well and I grabbed her. I was binding her legs together when she shouted something. I didn't hear what it was but suddenly that fairy Bluebell appeared and hit me with one of her spells. I didn't try to fight her because she might have captured me and found out about the mine, so I ran away.'

'But all is not lost,' said Demodus. 'When we try to capture her next time I have learned that the first thing we have to do

is to gag her as fast as we can and stop her from calling for help.'
'Divide and conquer,' Furnusabal, smirked an evil grin covering his ugly face.

Later that night, as Peggy lay fast asleep, she was completely unaware that already another evil plot was about to be hatched to capture her.

Chapter 4

PEGGY GOES FRUIT PICKING

Rose Goody was very busy, because ever since she began using her big new washing machine, more and more people seemed to be bringing their washing and ironing to her. She was really pleased because now with all the extra work she was able to save some of the extra money each week in the village bank. The bank manager, Mr Penny, was a nice man and had opened an account for her and her husband, George, when they first got married. He welcomed the news that she was busy, and showing a handsome profit. Soon perhaps she would be able to afford to pay someone to help her; the work load was becoming at times more than she could manage.

Peggy was doing most of the shopping for her mother now because she was so busy in the laundry, and today she was going to the greengrocer's shop. Rose had given her some money and a bag with two sturdy handles and off she went. On the way she met her friend, Cindy. 'Hello, Cindy,' she said, 'I'm going to the greengrocers. Would you like to come with me?' 'Great,' said Cindy, and taking Peggy's hand, off they went, swinging their arms as they walked.

When they arrived Peggy heard the greengrocer, Mr Sprout, talking to a customer. 'I'm sorry there are no apples or pears today because Farmer Oaks hasn't made his normal delivery like he should have.' 'Oh, well,' said the customer, 'I'll try again tomorrow.' 'Hello, Peggy,' said Mr Sprout, turning to her. 'I hope you haven't come for apples or pears, because Farmer Oaks hasn't delivered any today and he should have done. I do hope there's nothing wrong up there at the farm. It's so unlike him not to deliver when he's promised.'

'Would you like us to go up to Acorn Farm and see if he is all right?' asked Peggy. 'Would it be much trouble?' said Mr Sprout. 'It would put my mind at ease.' Peggy had brought a shopping list with her and asked Mr Sprout if he would put the vegetables on the list in her bag while they went to Acorn Farm. 'Of course I will,' he said.

Acorn Farm wasn't far away and they were there in no time. As they walked up the gravel path to the farm house, Henry, the farmer's dog came bounding towards them barking and pawing the ground, then ran towards the orchard. 'I think he's trying to tell us something,' said Peggy. 'Let's follow him,' and off they ran following Henry. When they reached the orchard they could see Farmer Oaks lying under an apple tree, and they ran over to him.

'Thank goodness you've come by!' said Farmer Oaks. 'I've been laying here for an hour or so. I slipped down the ladder and I think I've sprained my ankle, and haven't been able to get up again. I need to let Mr Sprout know—he'll be wondering where I've got to with his fruit delivery.' Peggy said 'We just came from there, and Mr Sprout asked us to come over and see if you were all right, and ask if you needed any help.' 'It certainly is good timing,' said Farmer Oaks. Cindy said 'I'll go and tell Mr Sprout what happened, and ask him to send some help,' and Peggy added 'I'll stay here and help Farmer Oaks.'

While Cindy was away Famer Oaks told Peggy how he would be in trouble now that he couldn't climb his ladder. 'I start picking the fruit from the bottom of the tree so I don't damage the fruit with the ladder when I climb up, and now because of this all the remaining fruit is at the top of the trees and I can't get to it.' 'Well,' said Peggy, 'I can pick it for you if you let me.' Farmer Oaks said, 'I couldn't possibly let you go up into the tree on a ladder; it's far too dangerous for a young girl.' 'I don't need a ladder!' laughed Peggy, 'Watch me! UP-UP,' said Peggy, and up she shot to the top of the apple tree where she picked two shiny red apples. 'DOWN-DOWN,' she called, and stood in front of Farmer Oaks with an apple in each hand and said, 'Like this.'

Farmer Oaks rubbed his eyes, not really believing what he had just seen. 'You must be Leggy-Peggy, the girl that saved young Stamp from the post office fire. I heard about it but now I've seen it for myself, you really do have magic legs. Well, I never,' he said. 'Have you got a basket I can use?' asked Peggy. 'Yes, over there by the cart,' said Farmer Oaks, pointing to a cart that was a quarter full of apples that had been picked before the accident. Peggy moved it closer to the apple tree, said 'UP-UP,' and started to pick the apples. By the time Cindy returned with help, Peggy had almost filled the cart to the top with lovely red apples.

Doctor Wells had brought Cindy back in his red sports car. He parked it in the farm yard, and walked over to Farmer Oaks. 'You are getting too old to climb about in trees, you know,' he said. 'Now, then, let's see what you've done to yourself.' They helped the farmer into the house and sat him down. 'You don't seem to have broken anything,' said Doctor Wells, 'but you have twisted your ankle quite badly, and you have a nasty swelling. Have you got any ice in the house? I need you to put some around your ankle.' 'Yes, there is some in the refrigerator in the kitchen,' said Farmer Oaks, 'Would you go and get it for me, Peggy?' Peggy went to the kitchen, where there was a big wide refrigerator standing in one corner. She opened the door to the freezer and took out two trays of ice. 'Will this be enough?' she said, passing the trays to Doctor Wells. He put the ice into a towel and wrapped it around Farmer Oaks' ankle. 'I want you to keep this on and stay in that chair until I come back in about an hour, and then I can put a bandage on when the swelling has gone down. Now I must get on.' Doctor Wells said his goodbyes and left. Farmer Oaks looked at Peggy and Cindy. 'You have helped me so much today I can't thank you enough, but I'm going to need some help picking the rest of my fruit. There are apples, and pears and plums to be picked. Would you both like to help me and earn yourselves some pocket money?' he asked. 'Yes!' said the girls at the same time. 'But you'll have to ask your parents first.' Peggy said 'I have got to go back to the greengrocers to do some shopping for my mother. Can we take some apples and pears back to the shop for you?' 'That would be a great help to me and would keep Mr Sprout happy until tomorrow.'

They both set off carrying a bag of apples and pears, and when they got back to the shop Mr Sprout was delighted with them. Cindy gave Mr Sprout the whole story and said Doctor Wells was going back to see Farmer Oaks later and he was not to worry himself. Peggy filled her order and the girls started to walk back home.

The next day the girls turned up at the farm ready for work. Peggy was up and down the trees on her magic legs and Cindy was emptying the baskets and giving the empties back to Peggy. They worked hard and three days later the fruit was picked, and Farmer Oaks was delighted. 'You've saved my bacon,' he said, 'Now let's go to the house and I can settle up with you.' They sat around the big wooden table and Farmer Oaks opened an old tin box, and inside were two stacks of notes. He picked up one of the stacks and counted out twenty five pounds for each of the girls. Peggy looked at Cindy, who was staring at the money with her mouth wide open, 'That's a fortune!' said Peggy, and Cindy just nodded without saying anything. 'You've earned every penny of it,' said Farmer Oaks, 'and there is a bag of fruit by the door for each of your mothers.' The girls thanked Farmer Oaks and started down the lane on their way home.

As they reached the end of the lane, a loud familiar voice said, 'Been picking fruit have we?' It was Andy Roughton the village bully, and on each side of him were his bully friends Josh Spittle and Bob Snipe. 'I could use some fresh fruit,' he growled. And turning to friends said 'How about you, lads?' His face was twisted in a menacing grin. 'Yeh—Yeh,' they said, like a pair of puppets. 'Hand it over, Goody,' he snarled. 'No chance,' replied Peggy, and Bully Roughton lunged toward her, but he was too slow. 'UP-UP!' shouted Peggy, and in an instant she towered above him. She took out a large apple from the bag and sent it crashing down on his head. He screamed in pain and his hands shot up to protect himself. He was much too late and a second apple hit him in the middle of his head. He didn't wait for a third, and took off like a wild horse with his two bully friends in close pursuit. 'DOWN—DOWN,' said Peggy, and as she came back to normal, she looked over at Cindy and said 'I don't think he likes my apples very much.' They started to laugh and didn't stop until they got home.

'Have you had a nice day?' asked Peggy's mother. 'Oh, it's had its ups and downs,' she replied, and they both stood there laughing. 'A day to remember,' thought Peggy.

Chapter 5

THE BABY LAMB

Peggy had been very busy all morning helping her mother clean the cottage windows. Ever since the Silver Fairy gave Peggy her magic legs she had been given the job of cleaning the upstairs windows. Peggy didn't mind, she loved to help her mother with the housework whenever she could. Today she was very excited, because Peggy and Cindy had been invited to Woollies Farm to see the new baby lambs.

Farmer Woolly was one of her mother's laundry customers, and he often had a chat with Peggy, and they got on very well together. The day before, Farmer Woolly had been collecting his laundry from the cottage, and while he was there he told Peggy all about the new lambs that had been born on the farm in the last few weeks and Peggy was fascinated by the news. There was one little baby lamb whose mother for some reason had refused to feed him, and so Farmer Woolly and his wife had to take it in turns to feed him with milk from a baby's bottle. It was when she was talking to Farmer Woolly he had said that if she would like to come up to the farm, he would let her feed the baby lamb and, what's more, he invited her to bring a friend. And so of course she had asked Cindy, and Cindy had said yes.

Peggy had just finished her lunch, when Cindy arrived. 'Are you ready, Peggy? I can't wait to see the baby lambs. I'm so excited,' she said, with a big grin on her face. 'I'm going up to Woollies Farm to see the baby lambs now,' Peggy said to her mother. 'Don't leave it too late coming home, will you?' 'No,' said Peggy, 'I promise.' Rose had a rule: she didn't mind where Peggy and her friends went, as long as she was told where they were going.

So off they hurried, half walking and half running, chatting excitedly. They were soon at the farm, and Peggy knocked on the farmhouse door. Mrs Woolly, a rounded woman with a big smile and cheeks like two big shiny red apples, greeted them warmly. 'Come in,' she said, 'you've timed it just right. I've just made the feed up for the baby lamb, and I'm about to take it up to him. Come on, follow me.'

When they got to the shed where the lamb had been moved, it was making a little squeaky noise. 'He's hungry by the sound of him,' said Mrs Woolly, 'just listen to him!' Mrs Woolly sat Peggy and Cindy down and said, 'Now don't you be afraid if he wriggles, girls' and handed Peggy the baby bottle with the warm milk in it. 'You go first, and then let Cindy have a go.' The girls loved it, and thought the lamb was going to swallow the bottle it sucked it so hard. When they were finished Mrs Woolly said, 'Let's go back to the house. I've baked a cake especially for you, and I've got some freshly made lemonade.' The girls were tucking into their cake and lemonade when Farmer Woolly came in. 'I could do with some of that, Ma,' he said, and sat down with a large piece of cake and a mug of lemonade. 'How did it go, girls?' he said, laughing out loud. 'We loved it, Farmer Woolly,' they both said together, 'and we would love to see all the others in the field.' Yes, of course you can, my dears,' said Mrs Woolly, 'as soon as you've finished eating.'

'Come on then, girls, it's time to have a look at all the others,' said Farmer Woolly, and off they went. There seemed to be hundreds of them, all running and jumping around, and it was lovely to watch them all. Farmer Woolly was scratching his head and counting the mother sheep. He said, 'Girls, I'm afraid there's one of the mother sheep missing. I'm sure she was here this morning when I was here. Will you help me look for her? She has a blue mark on each front leg, so you can't miss her.' They searched all over but could not find her. Then, suddenly, they could hear Farmer Woolly shouting to them from the next field. They both ran towards his voice and saw Farmer Woolly looking down into the valley below. Somehow the fence had been broken and the mother sheep had wandered through and fallen, and as they looked down they could see she had tumbled over the edge and was wedged between the cliff face and a small tree jutting out. At any moment it looked as if the tree would give way and the sheep would fall to her death. Farmer Woolly had already started running back to get a rope, and when he returned he was puffing and panting. He had a large coil of rope over one shoulder, which he quickly unravelled and threw the end close to where the sheep had fallen. Then he picked up the end closest to him and tied it around the trunk of the nearest tree.

'Girls, will you watch this end of the rope for me? And make sure it doesn't come loose. I'm going to climb down the side of the cliff and tie the rope to the sheep and pull her back up.' He stood on the edge of the cliff and slowly began to drop down. When he was level with the mother sheep he tried to step onto the small tree that held her, but as soon as his weight went onto the trunk it began to bend. He moved away quickly, and knew he would not be able to get the rope around her. He could see that the tree was about to come loose and fall, so he turned and scrambled back up the cliff. There was very little time left. He thought, 'What am I going to do to save the mother sheep from falling to her death?' When he got back up to the top he felt very upset that he could not do anything to help his sheep. Peggy asked Farmer Woolly what was the matter. He explained to her that when sheep give birth, they are very weak and sometimes get careless.

'Every year at this time I lose one or two and never find them, so when I do find one I'm desperate to save her. But it looks as if she's going to fall any second.' When Peggy could see what was happening, she said 'I can do it if you let me,' and explained her plan. 'If you hold my feet I can stretch my legs until I am level with the mother sheep and because I have two hands free I can easily tie the rope around her, and together we can pull her back up to safety.' 'I don't know,' said Farmer Woolly, 'It sounds pretty dangerous to me.' 'Do we have any other choice?' asked Peggy, holding out her arms and shrugging. 'It will be safe as long as you hold me tightly, and it won't take me very long. Shall we do it?' 'Yes,' said Farmer Woolly, 'let's do it while we still have time.' He started to lower Peggy over the cliff and when she was dangling over she said 'UP-UP' and her legs went longer and longer until she was level with the sheep. She wound the rope around her three times, as she had been instructed, and then tied a knot at the end over the top. When she finished she said 'DOWN-DOWN' and her legs got shorter and shorter until she was back to the top of the cliff. Farmer Woolly pulled her back on top and sat her down. 'Well done, Peggy,' he said. 'Now let's see if we can all pull her back up to safety.' They pulled slowly and carefully and up she came. When she was safely back on top they untied the rope and the sheep ran back to the flock and her baby. 'Peggy, I can't thank you enough for what you have done here today,' said Farmer Woolly, 'or you, Cindy. You are both very brave girls and I intend to tell the whole village about you both.'

Down in the valley, directly below the tree where the mother sheep had been hanging on for dear life, was Furnusabal. He was stamping around in a fuming rage. 'That Peggy Goody has done it again!' he roared. 'Why can't she mind her own business?' he screamed at Yellow Flame and his band of Imps. They stood in silence looking at the ground, not daring to move or make a noise. This time every year, when the mother sheep are weak and easily frightened, Furnusabal positions a band of Imps up in the fields and when the farmer is not there keeping watch they single out the weakest one and drive her over the cliff edge. Today the plan had worked, but the small tree had got in the way. It would have been just a matter of time and the small tree would have given way letting the mother sheep fall to her death. They would carry her body to the Fire Pit and roast her over it, and have a real feast. But no, that meddling Peggy Goody with her magic legs interfered and ruined everything. Somehow she had to be stopped.

On the way home the girls couldn't stop talking about what had happened and what a great adventure they had had. 'See you tomorrow,' said Cindy. 'Bye,' said Peggy, and off home they went. Peggy recounted the whole story that evening. She told her mother every detail, and how Farmer Woolly had called them brave girls, and that he had said they could see the lambs any time they wished. Both girls slept well that night, both dreaming about feeding the baby lamb.

Chapter 6

PEGGY GOES FISHING

P eggy had been invited to go out for the day with Cindy and her mother and father. They were taking a trip out to a large lake, where Cindy's father liked to do some fishing. Peggy didn't know anything about fishing, or was especially interested, but any reason to spend the day with her best friend was a good enough reason, so a day's fishing was OK.

Cindy had been busy in the kitchen helping her mother put up a lovely hamper with all sorts of goodies in it for the girls, and Cindy's father was loading the car with his fishing tackle. 'All done,' he said. 'Is the hamper ready to load in?' 'Yes,' answered Cindy's mother, and handed it to him. He placed it carefully in the boot of the car and when everything was packed away, asked 'Are we all ready to go?' And so they got into the car and started off down the lane towards Peggy's house. As the car pulled up outside the cottage Peggy was waiting for them and jumped into the backseat next to Cindy. Cindy's mother got out and popped in to say hello to Rose, they had a brief chat, and then off they went.

The lake was about five and a half miles away, and Cindy's father had put down the car roof. It was lovely for the girls sitting with the wind blowing through their hair, and in what seemed to be no time at all they had arrived by the lakeside. It was a beautiful day, with the water sparkling in the sunshine, and the girls were very excited. They all got out and started to unload the car. Cindy laid out a big red tartan blanket on the ground, and her mother unpacked the hamper, with each plate covered with cling film to keep away flies or wasps from settling on the food. During the picnic preparations Cindy's father sorted out the fishing tackle and set it up by the lakeside, and within fifteen minutes he had settled himself down and ready for a good day's fishing.

While the girls were arranging everything, another car pulled up close by, with a small dingy-type rowboat on the roof rack. And as soon as the car stopped the passengers got out, and a young boy jumped from the backseat and started shouting and running about. He seemed to be very excited, and just a little bit naughty, because his mother asked him to stop making such a noise and consider other people, but he took no notice. The boy's father started to take the small boat from the car's roof rack. He placed it on the ground beside the lake, and then put two oars in the boat he had taken from the back of the car. He also had fishing tackle and it looked as if he intended to row out onto the lake and fish from the boat.

When everything had been laid out, Cindy's mother said they could play until lunch time, while her father was fishing and she would read her book. They did not need telling twice and off they went to have some fun. They had both brought their skipping ropes, and Cindy had a ball so they could play catch. They played and talked and then started to walk back to the car. They were both feeling quite hungry by now, and were looking forward to the special picnic Cindy's mother had prepared.

When they got back, Cindy's mother was taking the cling film off the plates of food. 'Just in time,' she said. 'Sit yourselves down and help yourself to whatever you fancy.' Cindy's father came up and was very quiet. Cindy's mother inquired about the type of bait he had been using. 'What are the fish taking today, love?' she asked, with a smile on her face. 'No notice!' he said, with a scowl, and sat down and started to munch on a sandwich.

When they had all eaten their fill, Cindy's mother suggested they relax and let their food go down before they started to run around again. They all lay back on the cool grass and closed their eyes. It was so peaceful. Suddenly, the silence was shattered. There was a loud shout from the car next to them, 'Come back here at once, you naughty boy!' Startled, they jumped up and could see that the young boy had climbed into his father's boat and pushed off out into the lake. He was waving one of the oars and laughing at his mother and father, and all the time the boat drifted further and further away from the bank. 'Come back here at once!' shouted his father, but the boy just laughed louder. Suddenly there was a scream, and without warning, the boat turned over and began to sink. The boy's mother yelled for help. 'He can't swim!' she cried. 'None of us can!'

Peggy was already in the water and as she waded deeper she was saying 'UP-UP.' She got to the boat just as it sank and grabbed the boy, but he was panicking, and kicking and thrashing with his arms. Peggy could not hold onto him. He slipped from her grasp and started to sink below the surface of the water. In the panic Peggy had swallowed a mouthful of water and was choking herself. Then, as she recovered, she desperately searched around but could not see the boy. He was under the water, but where? She knew she had only one choice. She would have to go under the water in one desperate effort to save him. She summed up all her strength and filled her lungs with as much air as she could breathe in, and said to herself 'DOWN-DOWN.' Fortune was on Peggy's side: the sun was shining brightly and its rays travelled deep into the water, where she could see the boy sinking slowly down. But Peggy was swimming down more quickly and, in an instant, she lunged out and grabbed his collar. 'UP-UP,' she said to herself, and the magic power in her legs shot her back up to the surface. 'Oh, no!' she screamed. She no longer was holding the boy, and her grip on his collar had slipped. He was still down there and must be drowning.

She shouted 'Blue Flash Help!' and Bluebell was there immediately, by her side.

And just as Peggy quickly explained the emergency Bluebell made a circling gesture with her hands and what looked like a glass bowl covered Peggy's head. 'This will let you breath under water,' she said. 'I've sent one down to the boy so he can breathe, too. He is unconscious, but alive, and we were just in time. I must warn you, Peggy, it's a bad time to be under the water. The Scaleygill People are down this end of the lake today. They have come to harvest the grasses that grow here. This is the shallowest part of the lake where the sunshine can reach down and make them grow, and they come here twice each year. They are very dangerous in large numbers and could hold you down, so please be careful, I can't come under the water to help you. Now go and get the boy and bring him back to the surface where he will be safe.'

'DOWN-DOWN,' said Peggy, as she went, again, below the surface. Down in the underwater grass she could see hundreds of fish-like creatures swimming around the boy. They looked like lizards about half a meter in length, but instead of front legs they had arms and hands and their heads were almost human but their eyes were glazed and their ears were flat and long like the gills on a fish. As Peggy moved towards them they scattered, and she started to untangle the boy's legs from the grass. She was aware that the Scaleygills were coming in greater numbers and they were all around her, their bulging eyes staring at her menacingly, slowly circling around them both. Peggy looked at the boy—his eyes were closed but he was breathing. She pulled at the grass and it came away from his legs. He was wearing a belt so she put her fingers around it and got a firm grip. She knew there would not be a second chance. 'UP—UP,' she said, and much more slowly than normal, she pushed her way through the Scaleygills and up to the surface of the lake. She turned around and started back to the shore, but it was hard work. The Scaleygills were so large in number it felt as though she was wading through a pool of treacle, and as she was going along she was saying 'DOWN-DOWN' and finally, at last, she was back to the shore.

The glass spheres had disappeared from their heads, but the boy's eyes were still tightly closed. His father reached down and took his son from Peggy. 'He's not breathing!' he screamed. Cindy's father leapt forward and took the boy from his father, laid him on the grass, and started to press down on his chest, again and again. Suddenly the boy coughed and water gushed from his mouth. He was alive! The boy cried for his mother, and she picked him up in her arms, where he clung to her as if he would never let her go. 'I'm sorry,' he cried.

It was a lesson the boy would never forget and neither would his parents. Not only had he nearly drowned, but he had lost his father's boat and all his fishing tackle, just because he had been naughty and would not listen to his parents. The boy's father came over to Peggy to thank her for what she had done. 'I've heard the stories about you, Peggy Goody, and how brave you are. Now I have seen for myself just how wonderful your gift is, and how you care for others. You risked your own life to save my son and I thank you from the bottom of my heart.' He turned away from Peggy, and went over to Cindy's father and said. 'I owe you a debt of gratitude for giving me back my son.' 'There is no debt owed,' said Cindy's father, 'but before you go, may I suggest that you take yourself and your family to first aid lessons, and also to swimming lessons, and until you have all learned to swim, forget about replacing your boat.' The man looked at Cindy's father and said, 'That is one piece of advice I will certainly be taking.' He shook his hand, then turned and walked away.

'Well,' said Cindy's mother, 'that's about as much excitement as I can take for today!' and began to pack away. Bluebell had cast a time delay spell over everyone while Peggy was under water, so no one realised how long she had taken, and with a wave of her hand she removed the spell and disappeared. Cindy was helping Peggy to dry off, but Peggy felt drained of energy and just lay back in the sunshine while everything was packed and put back in the car.

Poor Cindy's father—he never got the chance to catch his fish. He puffed out his cheeks and gave out a big sigh, 'Ah, well, there's always another day,' and they all burst out laughing. If only he knew what was really out there in the lake grass, but then again he never would. Peggy had entered into a very strange world indeed. On the way home Cindy said to Peggy, 'Well, that wasn't as boring as we thought it would be, was it?' and they laughed all the way back home.

Chapter 7

THE SAFARI PARK

Rose Goody was very excited because today she would be the proud owner of a large tumble drier. She had been working so hard over the past six months, and now all her efforts were being rewarded. Peggy asked her mother what time it was being delivered. 'Any time now,' replied her mother, and as soon as she had said it, Mr Sparks' van pulled into the yard. It came to a halt and he got out. 'Good morning, ladies, how are you both today?' 'Better for seeing you,' said Rose, giving him a big smile.

'I've brought your new tumble drier, so if you just show me where you want it, Mrs Goody, you can leave it to me, and you'll be all fixed up and running in no time at all.'

'Mr Sparks, can I come and watch while you fix it in, please?' asked Peggy. 'Yes,' he said smiling, 'you can come and keep me company.' Mr Sparks unloaded the machine and set about wiring it up. It didn't take long and when he had finished he asked Rose to try a load of washing to make sure it was dry enough, and then he made sure she knew how to work it. The first load came out and was bone dry. Rose was delighted. 'This will save me so much time. Thank you, Mr Sparks.' 'The pleasure is all mine,' said Mr Sparks, and loaded his tools into the van. Then, just as he was about to leave, he suddenly remembered.

'Peggy, I've got a message for you from Mrs Stamp. She'd like you to pop into the post office today if you can, because she has something to ask you. I can give you a lift down there now if you like. I'm going there next to fit some smoke alarms.'

Peggy turned to her mother and asked if she could go with Mr Sparks. 'Yes, of course you can,' she said. 'Good,' said Mr Sparks, 'jump in, Peggy, and we'll be off.' They arrived at the post office while Mrs Stamp was serving a customer and when she had finished, she turned and said hello to Peggy and Mr Sparks. 'Peggy, would you mind going through to the living room? Billy's in there. I just want to show Mr Sparks where I want him to put the smoke alarms.'

After the fire at the post office Mr Stamp realised how dangerous it was not to have smoke alarms fitted in the house, and he knew that if Peggy had not been there on the day of the fire well, goodness knows what might have happened to little Billy. As soon as Mrs Stamp finished instructing Mr Sparks, she came to see Peggy in the living room. 'Peggy, how would you like to spend a day with us at the Safari Park? We would love you to come with us. It's tomorrow so we need to know as soon as possible.' 'Oh yes, I would love to, but I'll have to ask my mother's permission first,' Peggy quickly replied. 'Of course,' said Mrs Stamp. 'Would you like me to phone her while you're here?' Peggy blushed with embarrassment. 'We don't have a telephone,' she said. 'It's the next thing on mother's list. She just bought a tumble drier, so she can't afford one yet.' 'I'm sorry,' said Mrs Stamp, 'I didn't think. Look. I'll take you home and we can ask your mother, and if you can go, I can come back and organise it all.'

On the way home Peggy was very excited. She had never been to a zoo let alone a Safari Park. 'Oh,' she thought, 'I do hope mother says I can go'. She need not have worried. Her mother agreed right away. 'How much do you need to get in?' she asked Mrs Stamp. 'Nothing,' said Mrs Stamp, 'it's our way of saying thank you to Peggy for saving our Billy.'

The next morning Peggy was up early. She was so excited and couldn't wait to see all those wild animals she had only ever seen pictures of in books at school.

Peggy sat with Billy in the back of Mr Stamp's car on the way there, and Billy said, 'Shall we play "I spy with my little eye?" And in no time at all they were at the entrance of the Safari Park. Mr Stamp bought the tickets and they were on their way. At first they drove through the area where the monkeys lived, and they were jumping on the car and looking at them through the windscreen. Suddenly, Peggy's blood ran cold. Staring directly at her through the side window of the car was a Demodom! How could they possibly have known she would be here today? Unknown to Peggy the Demodoms had aided Furnusabal with the fire at the post office. The Demodoms had dug a tunnel from the forest directly underneath the post office so the Fire Imps could get there without being detected. Once in place, they had caused the fire, fanned the flames, and created thick black smoke to confuse the fire service when they arrived, so they could go about their evil plan to capture Billy Stamp's soul. But for Peggy and Bluebell's intervention they would have succeeded.

So it was just by chance that Demodus had sent one of his Demodoms down the tunnel that led to the post office to make sure it was sealed off properly and would not be discovered by the humans. The Demodom had arrived underneath the post office at the same time Mrs Stamp was asking Peggy to go to the Safari Park. He had made sure the tunnel was secured, and dashed back to the mine to tell his master what he had overheard. 'Well done!' roared Demodus, an evil grin spreading over his ugly face. 'Perhaps we can arrange a little surprise for Miss Goody and her friends.'

Peggy felt very uncomfortable and was glad when the car had passed through the monkey section. Had she just imagined it? She wasn't at all sure. 'Forget it,' she told herself. 'Enjoy the day.' And as they moved on they saw lions and tigers, elephants and rhinos, and a big pool with hippos diving under the water and back up again. Then they came to the giraffes, but something was going on. The gamekeepers were looking up at one of the giraffes and pointing at its head. It seemed to be in pain.

They all got out of the car and Mr Stamp asked one of the gamekeepers what was wrong. 'He's got a large thorn in the side of his face,' he said, 'and we can't get up to him to pull it out, and don't really want to give him an anaesthetic and knock him out if we can think of another way of getting it out, but we are very worried it might get infected.'

'Can I help?' asked Peggy. 'I could get up and pull it out.' 'And what makes you think you can do any better than us, young lady?' said the gamekeeper, looking at her with a disbelieving smile. 'I'm Peggy Goody, and I can reach up to him and pull out the thorn and put a dressing on at the same time if you want me to.' The gamekeeper looked at Mr Stamp. 'Do you think that she could really do it?' 'Oh yes,' said Mr Stamp confidently. So the gamekeeper gave Peggy a pair of rubber gloves, instructing, 'Please put these on. And now I want you to listen to me very carefully. If at any time you feel in danger I want you to come down immediately. Is that understood?' 'Yes,' answered Peggy. She had been given a large pair of tweezers and a dressing with sticky tape on the sides. She stood close to the giraffe, and said 'UP-UP,' and when she was level with his head she could see the thorn sticking out of his cheek. She gently stroked him, and whispered, 'Don't be afraid. I've come to help you.' Carefully she took the tweezers and held them over the thorn. She gripped as hard as she could and pulled. The thorn came out clean, and the giraffe jerked his head in pain. Peggy held herself up as the giraffe's head came back, and Peggy was able to put the dressing over the hole that thorn had made. The giraffe was very gentle with Peggy. He looked at her with big brown eyes, and licked her arm, as if to say thank you for helping me. Peggy stroked his head and said, 'I hope you get better soon.'

Suddenly there was a loud scream. 'The rhino's got out of his pen and he's charging this way!' From where Peggy was she could see the rhino coming closer. 'Get back into the car!' she shouted to the Stamps. 'I'll be all right!' They rushed back into the car just as the rhino thundered past them. Peggy had moved away from the giraffe, and as the rhino charged straight for her she opened her legs and it ran right through. But it wasn't about to give up and turned back around in a cloud of dust and charged at Peggy again. She only just managed to open her legs in time and let the rhino go thundering through, but it would not miss again. 'Blue Flash Help!' she cried out loud in a frightened voice. And suddenly Bluebell was by her side. She pointed her wand at the rhino. 'Stopellus!' she shouted, and the rhino stopped dead in its tracks. Within minutes two gamekeepers had ropes around the rhino and were leading him back to his pen. Bluebell turned to Peggy. 'You should be safe now. This is the work of Demodus and his Demodoms, so stay alert' and with a blue flash disappeared. Peggy said 'DOWN-DOWN,' and she was back to her normal size again. Everyone was clapping and shouting. 'Well done! I've never in all my time at the park seen anything like that before,' said the head gamekeeper. 'How ever can we repay you, err, Leggy—Peggy?' The giraffe bent down and licked Peggy on the arm again; she laughed and walked back to the car. On the way home they couldn't stop talking about all the wonderful animals they had seen and, of course, Peggy's adventure with the rhino and the giraffe.

Two days after Peggy's trip to the Safari Park, she was sitting in the garden with her mother having a cup of tea, when a van with ladders on the roof pulled up outside the house. Peggy looked at her mother. 'Who can this be?' 'I don't know,' said her mother. A man got out of the van and walked towards them. 'Mrs Goody?' the man enquired. 'Yes,' said Rose, 'may I help you?' 'Yes, I'm a telephone engineer and I've come to install a new telephone for you, courtesy of the Safari Park. There is nothing to pay, because it has all been taken care of by them.'

Unknown to them, Mrs Stamp had told the head gamekeeper at the Safari Park that if he meant what he said about repaying Peggy for her help then getting a telephone installed for them would be a wonderful way because Peggy's mother could not afford one for themselves. 'Leave it with me,' he had said, and here it was.

'I don't know what to say,' said Rose. 'Heaven knows I can certainly use it.' When the man had finished he showed Peggy and her mother how to use it and left them with a book of instructions. Peggy was so excited. 'Please, can I phone Cindy and tell her?' she asked. 'Yes, of course you can, and I can watch what you do.' Peggy made their very first phone call from their cottage. One hour later the telephone rang for the first time. Peggy's mother picked it up. 'Hello,' she said, 'this is Rose Goody speaking.' She felt so important, and she was shaking with excitement. It was the head gamekeeper from the Safari Park. He introduced himself and asked if everything was to her satisfaction. 'Oh yes,' she said, 'thank you so much.' 'Mrs Goody, you have a very special kind and loving daughter, and I will always remember what my mother used to say to me: that goodness sometimes has a strange way of rewarding you. I hope you and Peggy have a pleasant evening, and I wish you good fortune. Goodbye.' and the line went dead. Peggy's mother replaced the phone, and stood quite still thinking about what had just been said to her. She looked over at her daughter, she looked so grown up and beautiful, more than she could have ever wished for, and she was indeed blessed.

In the depths of the forest the noise of cursing could be heard coming from the mine. Demodus was in an angry rage. 'What have we got to do to win? My plan was executed to the letter, and I am not blaming you this time,' he said, waving his claw like hand at his Demodoms, who were sitting cross legged in front of him. 'No, we have to find a way to separate her from that fairy Bluebell. Another day—another day,' he said to himself, and drifted off into a different train of thought. The Demodoms got to their feet and quietly disappeared.

Chapter 8

THE LIGHTHOUSE KEEPER

Peggy and Cindy were on their way home from school. At last it was Friday afternoon and they were looking forward to the weekend. Rose had arranged a trip to the seaside on Sunday, and Cindy was going to go with them. They walked along talking excitedly about all the things they would do when they got there, and when they arrived at Cindy's house, Peggy gave Cindy a hug and said, 'I'll see you on Sunday morning. We'll pick you up at 9.' Rose had arranged for Mr Miles, the village taxi driver, to take them there and pick them back up at 6.00 pm. It was twelve miles to the coast so it would not take very long, and they could spend a full day there.

When Peggy got home her mother had the evening meal almost ready. She went and washed her hands and face, and laid the table out for her mother and herself. Friday night was fish night, and Rose had bought two pieces of cod loin from Mr Gill, who owned the fishmongers in the high street. They were having it with potatoes mashed with butter, peas, and parsley sauce—it was one of Peggy's favourite meals, and she always left a clean plate.

After the dishes were washed and put away, Peggy settled down with her mother and talked about the things that had happened during the day. Peggy said how happy Cindy had been when she had asked her to go to the seaside with them, and to thank her for being invited. Rose smiled, 'Well, you've certainly been on enough trips with Cindy and her parents.'

When Rose had been in the village earlier that day she had purchased the food for their packed lunch on Sunday, and she planned to prepare it Saturday evening in readiness for an early start the following morning. They both had a busy Saturday ahead, and Sunday would be a nice relaxing change.

'Sunday morning, at last!' thought Peggy. She had been awake for ages, and guessed that Cindy had been, too. She was washed and dressed and had finished her breakfast in record time, and was ready and waiting at the door. Mr Miles pulled up outside the house at precisely 8.30, and in a cheerful voice said, 'Are you all ready to go, ladies?' He winked his eye at Peggy, and she giggled excitedly. They were soon at Cindy's house, and she was already waiting for them. When they were all in the car and on the way, the girls began talking and didn't stop until the car came to a halt at the seaside. 'We're here,' said Mr Miles.

Rocky Point was well known for its lighthouse. It stood at the end of a fierce looking finger of rocks that stretched out to sea some one hundred and fifty metres.

Before the lighthouse was built, there were tales of smugglers who waited for ships to crash onto the rocks. They would row out in their boats and steal the cargo from the wrecks and bring it back to Sandy Cove, where it would be sold and moved on.

Sandy Cove was a small inlet, with ninety steep steps that wound down from the car park on the main coast road to the beach. It would be hard work carrying the bags down to the shore, but well worth the effort. It had soft sand and was sheltered from the wind, a perfect place for a picnic. When the taxi was unloaded they said goodbye to Mr Miles, and started down the steps. 'Be careful, girls,' said Rose, 'and no running.'

The girls spent the next three hours exploring the small caves in the rocks and making up stories about smugglers and hidden treasure. Cindy found a small rock pool close to the sea where rock crabs had made their home, and as they watched them walking under the water, Peggy said they must be able to breath under water like fish. They both jumped and looked up at the same time—Rose was calling out for them to come and have something to eat and drink. 'When we have finished our lunch and had a rest, would you like to go and visit the lighthouse?' 'Yes!' said the girls, both at the same time. Then they looked at each other and burst out laughing.

Rose had been to the lighthouse many times when she was a little girl, and she knew the keeper Jake Beam. Locally he was known as Old Jake, and the story was that he had lived there since he was a boy.

As soon as the girls were finished they started to pack away and tidy everything up. They collected all the rubbish in a plastic bag and tied it at the top ready to throw into the waste bin in the car park at the top of the steps. They made their way up the steep and winding path, and as they reached the top were gasping for breath. 'How hard was that?' asked Cindy. Peggy and her mother just nodded their heads.

After they got their breath back and had thrown the rubbish into the bins, they started toward the lighthouse, a further half a mile down the coast. When they arrived they had to walk down a narrow path on the rocks that led out into the sea. It had ropes running down each side to hold on to, and ran all the way down to six large stone steps that led up to a heavy oak door. Today the weather was warm and dry, but on a wet and windy day you would be holding the ropes to stop yourself falling into the sea.

When they arrived at the end of the path, they could see a small crowd of people standing on the steps by the lighthouse door. 'Whatever can be the matter?' said Rose, looking concerned. 'I hope Old Jake isn't poorly. Come on, girls, let's find out what's going on.' And as they got closer they could hear people calling out to Jake. Rose asked what happened and a lady standing next to her said, 'It's Old Jake. We've been trying to get him for the past five hours and he's not answering the door, and the door is locked and bolted from the inside. The police have been but it's impossible to get ladders up on the rocks, so they have asked the coast guard to help, but their helicopter is six miles up the coast, where they're busy helping the crews from off two boats that collided, and they've reported one of them was sinking.'

Rose turned to Peggy, 'Do you think you could reach the balcony that runs around the top of the lighthouse? It's a long way up, so don't be afraid to say no.' Peggy did not even hesitate. She stood as close to the lighthouse wall as she could and took a deep breath. 'UP-UP,' she said, and her magic legs shot her high into the air. As soon as she was level with the iron rails, she realised that she had a problem. She was high enough but because the lighthouse was smaller at the top she was some two metres away from the rails that ran around the top. She thought for a moment, then decided she would have to rock forward and backward, until she was close enough to grab hold of the rail. It was a bad decision. She was fifty metres up in the air, and the smallest gust of wind could tip her over.

She started to rock forward and backward and then it happened, and she was suddenly falling backwards towards the sea. 'Blue Flash Help!' she screamed, and from out of nowhere a flock of seagulls flew into her path, lifted and pushed her towards the hand rails, and Peggy grabbed them with both hands. She had never been this high before and could feel the wind tugging at her. Peggy was terrified, and leaned right over the rail, saying 'DOWN-DOWN.' Her legs came back up to her, and she pulled herself over the rail and sat on the balcony floor gasping for breath. She was aware that Bluebell was standing next to her, but she did not have the normal smile on her face, and she let Peggy know how cross she was with her. 'That was a very silly thing to do,' she said in a frosty voice. 'You could have killed yourself. Jake would still be locked in and you would have been dead. What would that have achieved?' 'I'm sorry,' said Peggy, feeling guilty, 'but I didn't think.' Bluebell said, 'You are a very brave young lady, and we all love and respect you for that. Your desire to help people in distress is a wonderful quality, but if you do things without giving any thought to it, you not only endanger yourself but others around you. Now, no one will be aware of what has just happened, so carry on into the lighthouse and find out what has happened to Jake.' Then, with a blue flash, she was gone.

Peggy stood up slowly on the balcony for a few moments to get her balance back, and as soon as she felt safe began to move around looking for a door. She found one and slid it open and, with a sigh of relief, stepped inside out of the wind. She was shaking; what had just happened really frightened her. 'What a fool I am,' she thought to herself, 'I could have easily gone back down and asked for a rope.' She was standing in the room where the light beamed out its warning, and in the floor was the trap door with an iron ladder leading down to where Jake lived. Carefully, she went down the iron ladder into the room below, and leading from there was a staircase. Peggy followed the stairs down, and at the bottom lay an old man. He was not moving but was breathing. 'It must be Jake,' she thought, 'he must have fallen down the stairs and knocked himself out.'

Peggy did not waste any time. She ran past him and down the next flight of stairs as fast as she could and they seemed to go down forever. When she got to the door she pulled back the two large bolts, turned the key in the lock, and with all her strength pushed it open. The people standing outside went wild shouting and clapping and cheering and calling out her name. Peggy's face was bright red—she was so embarrassed, but it seemed her reputation was spreading.

In the meantime a doctor had arrived and rushed up to help Jake, and when he came down he said that Jake was going to be all right. He had slipped on the stairs, fallen and bumped his head. 'He's asking to see the girl who helped him,' said the doctor. 'Would you be kind enough to go and see him?' Peggy entered with her mother and they climbed up the stairs to see Jake, and when he saw Peggy's mother he was really surprised. 'Rose! Well, I never, and is this Peggy, your daughter? What a small world we live in. Peggy, I want to thank you so much for what you did today. It takes a very special person, who puts herself in danger to help others like you have, and you are certainly one of those. God bless you. Now then, Rose, tell me what you've been up to since I last saw you.'

Rose asked Peggy to go and look after Cindy while she had a quick word with Jake. She did not want to talk about Peggy's father in front of her. After a while they said their goodbyes and left the lighthouse, and walked back along the rocks to the road, toward the car park. On the way back they talked about Old Jake. He told them to come back when they could and he would show them how everything worked, and afterward they would have tea with him in the lighthouse. Cindy said, 'I can't wait to get back home and tell Mom and Dad what happened today.' If only she knew the true story but, once again, it would be a secret between Bluebell and Peggy. 'Will we be able to come back real soon, Mrs Goody?' asked Cindy. 'Yes, of course,' said Rose.

Mr Miles was waiting for them when they arrived at the car park. 'Have you had a good day, ladies?' enquired Mr Miles, and gave them a wink and chuckled. 'Eventful, to say the least,' replied Rose. They got into the taxi and started the journey home, and on the way Rose explained to Mr Miles what had happened at the lighthouse. 'Goodness me,' he said, 'how brave of you, Peggy.' 'It was nothing, really,' said Peggy, blushing with embarrassment. 'Well,' said Mr Miles, 'it will make a good story for me to tell my passengers tomorrow.' Mr Miles dropped Peggy and her mother off first because Cindy's house was on his way home. Cindy said, 'Goodbye, I'll see you at school tomorrow, Peggy,' and off they went. The girls slept well that night, dreaming of smugglers and shipwrecks and caves and, of course, of Old Jake and the lighthouse.

Chapter 9

THE GOLDEN FAIRY QUEEN

Peggy woke up with a start. Someone was calling her name. She rubbed her eyes and peered into the darkness of her room. Sitting at the bottom of her bed, bathed in a pale blue light was Bluebell. 'Hello, Peggy,' she said, smiling at her. 'I hope I didn't frighten you.' Peggy smiled back at her. 'No, you didn't,' she said, pulling back the bed clothes and sitting up on the side of the bed. 'It's really lovely to see you again. Why have you come? I didn't call for you in my sleep, did I?'

'No, you have not called,' she replied. 'I have been sent here by the Silver Fairy. She would like you to meet with her tomorrow in the Silver Cave. She told me to tell you it is something very important, and it will take up most of the day. You will have to ask your mother's permission first, of course, and if she agrees, I will be by the great oak tree at the edge of the forest at 9 tomorrow morning.'

Peggy said she would be delighted to go with her, and was certain her mother would give her permission. 'Good,' said

Bluebell. 'I hope to see you in the morning then.' and disappeared in a flash of blue light.

Peggy found it hard to go back to sleep. Had she somehow done something to upset the Silver Fairy? After all, Bluebell had said it was something very important, and she knew she had upset Bluebell the last time they met. Peggy wanted to wake her mother there and then and ask if she could go, but then realised it was the middle of the night and tomorrow was Sunday. And every Sunday Peggy's mother had an extra hour in bed. It was the only time she really had to herself, as the rest of the week she was busy with the laundry service. So Peggy waited until the early morning light streamed through her bedroom window and when she could wait no longer, got out of bed and went downstairs to the kitchen. She made a pot of tea, and poured a cup to take up to her mother.

'Good morning, mother,' she said, as she pushed open the door to her mother's bedroom. 'What time is it?' asked her mother, looking over at the alarm clock by the side of the bed. It was 7.00. 'Is everything all right?' she asked, looking up at Peggy and yawning. 'Yes,' Peggy reassured her. 'I've made you a cup of tea, and while you are drinking it I have something to ask you.' She told her mother of the visit from Bluebell last night and that she had asked to get her permission to visit the Silver Fairy. 'Can I go, mother? Please, can I go?'

'Yes, of course you can,' said her mother, 'but not until you have had a good breakfast.' Every Sunday morning Peggy and her mother had a cooked breakfast of bacon, eggs, baked beans and buttered toast. Peggy would lay the table while her mother did the cooking, and after that they would sit and chat.

But today was different. Peggy had only one thing on her mind, and it wasn't sitting around chatting. As soon as she and her mother finished eating she started to clear away. 'My goodness, you are in a rush,' said her mother. 'Look, you go and get ready and I'll finish up here.' Peggy didn't need telling twice and she ran upstairs to get ready.

'Be careful how you go in that forest,' shouted Rose, as Peggy went skipping down the path. She turned, smiled, and blew her mother a kiss.

As Peggy got up close to the great oak tree, she could see Bluebell sitting on one of the lower branches. 'Hello, Peggy. I'm so glad you could come,' she said, and floated down from the tree. 'Are you ready to meet the Silver Fairy? Because I know she is looking forward to seeing you again.' 'Oh, yes,' said Peggy, 'I'm very excited.'

'Right,' said Bluebell. 'Hold my hand and follow me.' As soon as she held Bluebell's hand she became invisible. 'Tell me if I go too fast,' said Bluebell, 'but we don't want to linger. There are Demodoms in the forest keeping watch, hoping you might wander into the forest on your own.' Bluebell was right. There were Demodoms hiding behind bushes and in trees. They seemed to be everywhere, their red eyes piercing through the gloom of the forest. 'How do they know I might be in this part of the forest?' asked Peggy. Bluebell said, 'Well, this is where you came into the forest when you rescued me from out of the tree, and I suppose they think you might come back. It is also where you became invisible to them, and maybe they are trying to pick up a scent that leads to the fairy site, but they're wasting their time because we didn't leave one.'

They sped through the woods and were soon standing at the fairy site. 'Follow me,' instructed Bluebell, and led Peggy to the entrance of the Silver Cave. To the human eye it was just another tree covered hill but, as Bluebell approached, it suddenly changed to an opening. They went inside and the Silver Cave appeared. It was dazzlingly beautiful: large crystal chandeliers hung from a silver roof, giving off a bright pure light, and there were hundreds of fairies all going about their different tasks. As they went deeper into the Silver Cave, Peggy could see the Silver Fairy sitting on a silver throne with pure white cushions and on each side was a silver chair also dressed in white. They approached the Silver Fairy and Bluebell announced Peggy's arrival. 'Thank you, Bluebell, that will be all for now.' Bluebell turned and flew away back to the woods.

'Peggy, you have grown since I saw you last.' 'Yes, I have,' said Peggy. I'm thirteen years old.' 'Ah!' said the Silver Fairy, smiling kindly at Peggy. 'A "Teenager" no less.' The Silver Fairy was much larger than the other fairies but she still only came up to Peggy's shoulders.

'We are going on a very special journey today, Peggy. Somewhere no other human has ever been before. We have been invited to visit the Golden Fairy Queen, in Ireland. I have arranged for my pilot to have my travel capsule ready to take us through the secret underground tunnel that leads to the Golden Cave. It will only take a minute to get there because the capsule travels by magic motion and is very fast.'

The capsule looked like a small rocket, round in shape with a pointed nose. The pilot was an older fairy. She opened up the top and they all got in. The pilot closed the top, secured it, and sat down at the controls. They started to move, but there was no sense of speed, and as soon as they had settled down the pilot announced their arrival.

The pilot opened the capsule and they climbed out. Peggy's heart was pounding. She was very nervous, and the Silver Fairy noticed. 'Please relax, Peggy. The Golden Fairy Queen is very wise and kind.' As Peggy entered the Golden Cave she was speechless. It was the most beautiful thing she had ever seen. Many times bigger than the Silver Cave, hundreds of gold and crystal chandeliers hung from the golden roof of the cave and their radiated sunlight made Peggy feel happy and warm. As they approached the throne room Peggy could see the Golden Fairy Queen sitting on a beautiful golden throne, decorated with cushions of finest scarlet velvet. On each side of the throne were further golden chairs, also arranged with scarlet cushions.

The Silver Fairy announced Peggy. 'Come and sit by my side,' said the Golden Fairy Queen. 'We have much to talk about.' She started by congratulating Peggy on her bravery and the maturity she had shown when tackling all the emergencies she encountered over the past year, with no concern for her own safety. 'And, Peggy, this brings me to the reason I have invited you here today.

'Both the Silver Fairy and I are worried that because of your concern for others you are putting yourself in danger and the possibility of seriously hurting yourself. Therefore, I must ask you if you want to keep your magic and all the responsibility that goes along with it. We realise it is a massive responsibility for one so young. The fairy world has never had a close relationship with a human as we have with you, and we have never passed on any fairy magic or given our trust to anyone from another group.'

Peggy looked at the Golden Fairy Queen and said, 'As long as I can help people I have no fear of personal danger, and I will use my gift to the best of my ability. I realise I have to be much more careful, and promise to "look before I leap" as my mother says I should.'

'I am pleased with your answer,' said the Golden Fairy, 'and I intend to keep you safe. The Silver Fairy and I have decided to extend your magic powers. From today you will possess enormous strength. It will be very difficult to hurt you, and you will be able to lift and move any heavy loads that stand in your way. We are facing perilous times, both in the fairy world and in yours. Evil is all around us, as you are beginning to find out for yourself, with the past events.

'Demodus is slowly regaining some of the magic he was stripped of when he was put on trial and exiled from the Great Cave in the land of Greco, by Igor King of the Gnomes. He has made a vow to damage the fairy world in any way he can as a vendetta against me, for capturing him when he was robbing the Rainbow Bank, and for handing him over to Igor. Furnusabal has promised to help him, and they have made a pact to work together in this aim.

'Peggy, you have upset both of them and they know you possess fairy magic and that Bluebell is your protector. They will do everything in their power to capture you and extract information about the fairy world. And because of this we will strengthen the non-remembrance spell we put on you for the location of the fairy site and the Silver Cave.

'Demodus has been mining tunnels in all directions hoping to find our network of transport tunnels. He will not have any success because of the Deflectus Charm we put on them, but as his own magic grows, who knows?

'These powers will be yours to use as you see fit, but you must at all times be extremely careful how and when you use them. Now, have you understood everything that I have said to you?'

'Yes,' said Peggy, still taking it all in. 'Thank you. I promise I won't let you down.' 'Is there anything you would like to ask me, Peggy?' said the Golden Fairy Queen.

'Yes,' said Peggy. 'I hope you don't think me rude, but why are all the fairies female?'

The Golden Fairy Queen smiled. 'What a good question to ask. Come, I will show you why.' She led Peggy to another Golden Cave, just off the main structure. 'This is where the fairy world all began.'

In the middle of the cave was a large golden tree where some of the older fairies were sitting caring for baby fairies. 'This is the Golden Birthing Tree, where all the fairies in the world begin their life. Fairies have no mother and father like humans; they are born of Mother Nature, and Mother Nature is born of Mother Earth, our whole makeup is female. Every ten thousand years the Birthing Tree gives birth to a new Golden Fairy Queen and a new Silver Fairy. Then it withers and dies. At that time the Silver Fairy and I will lie down where the Golden Birthing Tree had been and go to sleep. Our seeds will sink into Mother Earth and a new Golden Birthing Tree will grow and a new ten millennia of fairies will begin. This is how the fairies have survived for countless millions of years.'

Peggy was fascinated by the story, but felt that it was all a dream. The fact was that when she got home that is exactly what she would think it was, but a dream she would remember. The Golden Fairy Queen turned to Peggy. 'It is time for you to go home now. I hope that in some future time we will meet again. Peggy, please remember what I have said, and be very careful how you use your new powers. Good fortune in your endeavours. Goodbye.' 'Goodbye,' said Peggy, and bowed.

The Silver Fairy led Peggy back to the travel capsule and soon they were on their way to the Silver Cave, in England. When they arrived, the Silver Fairy summoned Bluebell. 'Please take Peggy back to the great oak tree and see her safely home.' The great oak tree would become a regular meeting place in future, because now it was the gateway to the fairy world for Peggy. Peggy said goodbye to Bluebell and started home. As she walked she wondered what adventures she would have with her new magic powers and how it might change her life. When she arrived home she told her mother of her new magic powers, but no matter how hard she tried she could not remember how she got them. She was firmly under a spell of Non-Remembrance.

Chapter 10
THE THUNDER STORM

All through the night the wind and the rain had been battering down on the cottage roof. At various intervals there would be a bright flash of lightning that would light up Peggy's room, then followed by a deafening clap of thunder. Her mother was down in the kitchen drinking a cup of tea because she couldn't sleep. Ever since she had been caught in a thunder storm when she was a little girl she had been frightened of thunder and lightning.

Peggy went downstairs to sit with her while the storm lasted. She couldn't sleep either, and as she sat down next to her mother she said, 'Don't worry, mother. I'll look after you and keep you safe.' Her mother smiled. She knew that if anyone could keep her safe it was her one and only Peggy. She was so proud of her daughter, and she had so many of her father's ways: kind, brave and a respect for others.

Rose Goody had never told her daughter how her father had died because she was just a baby at the time, but now she thought was probably the time. She said, 'Peggy, I want to talk to you about your father. I want you to know how brave he was and how he died while he was trying to save someone else.' Rose leaned forward and held Peggy's hand.

'It was one afternoon when your father was on his way home. It had started to rain, and the sky was turning dark and angry. A farmer from the next village had been visiting his sister in our village; the weather had been sunny when he started out and so he had decided to use his horse and carriage for the journey. When he was on his way home it had started to rain so he drove quicker as he went down the lane. There was a sudden flash of lightning and a roar of thunder. The horse panicked, reared up, and bolted, and the farmer was thrown to the back of the carriage and lost control. Your father was walking down the lane at the same time and when he saw what had happened he ran toward the horse and grabbed the reins, but the horse didn't stop and your father's hands slipped on the wet reins. The horse and carriage ran over him.'

Rose had tears in her eyes as she told her story. She said, 'The last thing your father said before he went to heaven was that he loved us both very much and he asked me to keep his little Peggy safe.'

Peggy looked at her mother. 'Thank you for telling me. You've more than kept your word. Nobody could have kept me safer or loved me more than you have, and now it's my turn to keep you safe.'

The storm rolled on through the night, and when the morning dawned it finally stopped. Peggy had slept the rest of the night in her mother's bed and when they got up her mother said, 'Thank goodness that's over. Let's go and have breakfast.'

When breakfast was over Peggy got herself ready for school, said goodbye to her mother, and off she went.

Just as she got to the high street she could see a crowd of people standing in front of the library. As she got closer she could see that the large horse chestnut tree which had stood in the high street for over a hundred years had been uprooted and crashed onto the library roof. The fire engine had arrived and the chief fire officer was directing his men to do various duties. Peggy walked over to the chief fire officer, and when he saw her he said, 'Hello, Peggy. I don't think you will be able to help me with this one. It's really tricky. Page Booker the librarian is trapped in her bedroom, and we are worried that if we force our way into the bedroom the roof might collapse and injure her. What we need is a crane big enough to pick the tree right up in the air, and then we could go in and get her out before anything collapses.'

'I can lift the tree up,' said Peggy, 'if you show me how you want it lifted.' The fire officer laughed out loud. 'I don't think so, Peggy. That tree must weigh over two tons.' Peggy looked him straight in the eye. 'Show me where you want it lifted to and if I can't do it, I'll just make myself look foolish.' The fire officer said, 'Have a go then, Peggy, but don't say I didn't warn you.'

He went up to the library and stood directly under the tree then pointed to a spot were the tree needed to be lifted. Peggy stood next to him and said 'UP-UP.' She shot up until her hands touched the tree. She closed her eyes and said to herself, 'I can do it. UP-UP,' and slowly the tree began to rise. She kept going until all the branches were free from the roof. Peggy slowly moved it onto one side and with the command 'DOWN-DOWN' carefully placed the tree on the ground.

When the tree began to move, the crowd gasped; they could not believe what they were seeing. The chief officer stood quite still, had he really seen young Peggy lift that massive tree? Suddenly, the crowd started chanting, 'Peggy Goody, Peggy Goody!' The chief officer wasted no time and jumped into action, shouting orders. 'Up the stairs, lads! Get Page Booker out of there and make it snappy!' Page lived alone and very rarely went out of the library other than to do her shopping, but she knew most of the people in the village because of her position in the library. So when she was brought out by one of the firemen everyone cheered, and they all crowded around to hear her account of what happened. She had been lying in bed listening to the storm when she heard a loud cracking sound. The tree had crashed through the ceiling of her bedroom, just missing her, and wedged the door shut trapping her inside.

Page was covered in dust and looked terrified. One of the firemen wrapped a large blanket around her to keep her warm, because she was only wearing a nightdress and a pair of slippers. After the accident had first happened Police Sergeant Charger had called for an ambulance. To make sure Page was all right they decided to take her to hospital to be checked, and as she was moved into the ambulance Sergeant Charger was scribbling in his notebook so as not to forget anything. But his mind was thinking about what he had just seen Peggy Goody do. It was quite impossible, but he had seen it with his own eyes. He knew he must talk to her, and find out how she had managed that remarkable rescue.

Peggy felt strangely relieved. She had practiced her new magic at home, lifting heavy objects like the washing machine and her mother's double bed, but nothing like the tree. It had been so easy, not that much effort at all. It was as if she had dreamed the whole thing. But she soon realised it was not a dream. Sergeant Charger put his hand on her shoulder and said, 'Peggy, I would like to have a private word with you, if I may.' 'Of course,' answered Peggy, and they moved to one side of the crowd, out of earshot.

'Peggy,' he said, 'I need to know how you lifted that tree. I have to write a report for the Chief Constable. Now, how can I put in my report that a young thirteen year old girl reached up and lifted a two ton horse chestnut tree from off a two storey building?' Peggy said, 'I've been given certain powers but I can't tell you where they came from or how I got them. But I do know this—they will only work if I use them for a good cause.'

Sergeant Charger scratched the back of his head while he tried to think of something to say. He gave a slight cough. 'I might have to call on you later to come down to the police station and have a talk with the Chief Constable.' Peggy asked if she could go, because she was late for school. 'Yes, yes,' said the Sergeant, looking rather flustered and waving his arms. 'Run along, run along.'

When Peggy arrived the news of her rescue had already reached the school, and children were lined up in the playground and as she walked in. They all clapped and chanted 'Leggy-Peggy, Leggy-Peggy!'

Later in morning Sergeant Charger arrived at the school and asked if he could take Peggy to the hospital to see Page Booker. She had been told what Peggy did and wanted to thank her personally. Stitchery Hospital, in Stonechurch, was six miles from school so Peggy sat back and enjoyed the ride. Sergeant Charger chatted and made small talk to make the journey more pleasant, when Peggy suddenly asked him, 'Did you know my father?' 'Yes, I did,' he said. 'Everybody did. George Goody was a friend to most folk in the village, and he always had a smile on his face, and a kind word for anyone that passed him by. A lot of the roofs in the village were thatched by your father and he was very proud of his work. It was a terrible shock to us all when George passed away, and you being just a baby made it very hard for your mother. But Rose soldiered on through it all and what a grand job she did with you, Peggy. You had a father to be proud of and I'm sure he would be just as proud of you.'

As they pulled up outside the hospital a crowd had gathered—some were nurses and some were from newspapers. Peggy was surprised. 'This could be tricky,' she thought. When she stepped from the car reporters surrounded her, shouting questions and pushing. Sergeant Charger put an arm around Peggy's shoulder and walked her to the entrance, and once inside things calmed down. There were two local newspapers in Stonechurch, the largest being The Daily News, and the other, Country Matters. Peggy sat on a chair, and answered the questions put to her by the reporters. After she had finished telling her story the reporters dashed off, while one of the photographers from the Daily News asked if he could have a picture of Peggy standing by Page's bed. 'Yes,' she said, 'if it is all right with Miss Booker' and off they went to see her. He took his photo and thanked them and left.

Peggy puffed her cheeks out and looked at the Sergeant. 'Alone at last.' 'I'm afraid this is something you'll have to get used to,' said the Sergeant. 'If you keep doing things like you have today the national press will be knocking on your door.'

Page Booker had been delighted to see Peggy. 'Thank you so much for saving me,' she said. 'I was terrified lying there in bed and was waiting for the roof to fall down on top of me. I will never be able to repay you.' 'You already have,' said Peggy. 'You're safe and sound, because if you weren't, where would I get my library books from?' They looked at each other and burst out laughing. They chatted for a while and then Sergeant Charger took Peggy back to school. At the end of the lessons, Peggy could not wait to get home and tell her mother all that had happened that day, and she ran all the way home.

Deep in the forest Furnusabal spoke to Demodus. They were digesting the news one of the Demodoms brought to them about Peggy Goody, and how she had single handed lifted a two ton tree off a two storey building. 'This is getting serious, now,' said Demodus. 'If she lifted a two ton tree, this means the fairies have given her more magical powers. But for what reason? Is it because we tried to capture her? If we try again she might be able to overpower and capture us. We must be very careful the next time we lay a trap for her.'

Furnusabal looked thoughtful. 'I think that there might be more to this than meets the eye,' he said. 'Listen to this and tell me what you think: The fairies can't go under water and survive, but we know that Goody can survive because of the incident in the lake, so she would be able to use fairy magic under water. Fairies are not allowed to enter human houses or buildings unless they have a human connection, but Goody can, and because of her fairy magic they could gain access to any building anywhere, and have the advantage of being invisible. With Goody, their power would increase enormously; and there would be no place to hide for the criminal and his friends.'

Demodus was deeply worried. His whole life was consumed with revenge against the fairy world for what they did to him. 'If this is true, he said, 'and I have to say it all makes sense, then we will have to be one step ahead of them all the time, and a lot of creatures will face fierce battles with the fairy world in future.'

Chapter 11

THE POWER COMPANY

Peggy arrived home from school, and as soon as she walked into the house she started chattering. She was so excited. Her mother looked at her and said, 'Peggy, you look all flustered. Whatever have you been doing?'

'I lifted a tree! I lifted a tree!' she said out loud. 'What do you mean, you lifted a tree?' asked her mother. 'Now come and sit by me and calm down.' She patted the cushion next to her on the sofa and Peggy sat down beside her. 'Now tell me what you've been getting up to.'

Peggy told her mother about the old horse chestnut tree, the library roof, and how she rescued Page Booker. She left nothing out, and included her visit to the hospital with Sergeant Charger to see Miss Booker, and how they had their photograph taken by The Daily News. When she had finished her story she took a deep breath. 'What do you think, mother?' Her mother looked at her in amazement. 'It sounds a bit like a fairy story to me.'

'Well, mother,' Peggy said, 'they did kind of help.' They looked at each other and laughed and hugged.

Suddenly the telephone rang and they both jumped. 'Who can that be?' said Rose, and picked it up. 'Hello, can I help you?' It was a man's voice. 'Is this Mrs Rose Goody?' 'Yes,' she replied. 'My name is Jack Flashman and I work for the Zeta Power Corporation. I would like your permission to come and see you right away. It is very urgent. I can explain the situation when I get there.'

'Well, I suppose so,' said Rose, with a surprised look on her face. 'Do you have my address?' 'Yes, thank you,' he said. 'They gave it to me at the police station. I'm on my way.'

'Who was that?' Peggy asked. 'A man from the Zeta Power Corporation. He said it was very urgent he speak with me. I can't think why. All our bills are up to date.'

Ten minutes later there was a knock on the door and when Rose opened it, standing there was a tall man. 'I'm Jack Flashman,' he said, holding out his hand. 'And I'm Rose Goody,' she said, shaking his hand. 'Please come in.' Peggy asked him if he would like a cup of tea. 'Yes, please,' he said.

'Now, Mr Flashman, how can I help you?' 'Please call me Jack,' he said smiling. 'Very well, and please call me Rose.'

'Well, Rose, it has come to our attention what your daughter Peggy did at the library today. Lifting that enormous tree, it was hard to believe and still is really, but Sergeant Charger said he saw it with his own eyes, and that is why I'm here, to ask for your daughter's help.

'We have a situation with several fallen trees that were blown down in the storm. In fact, six large trees are lying across overhead power cables at this moment, and they are threatening the power supply to Stitchery General Hospital. We have a team of men with chainsaws trying to clear them away, but it's taking far too long, and I hoped that somehow your daughter could help move them away from the power lines so we can restore them back to normal.'

Peggy stopped making the tea and listened. 'This is why I have been given my powers,' she said, and she knew what she must do. 'I'm sorry, mother, I've got to go right now and help. Mr Flashman will look after me.' She put her arms around her mother and hugged her. 'Don't worry. No harm will come to me.'

Peggy turned to Mr Flashman, 'I'm ready when you are.' He was on his feet and opening the door in a second. As Rose watched them drive away in a large Jeep she could not help feeling a little bit worried, but she knew Peggy was being watched over and kept safe.

Jack Flashman drove through Little Thatch and on towards Stonechurch Town. Half a mile before they reached the town he pulled over to a gate that led into the open fields. There were several vans with flashing orange lights, and men standing in groups, talking and pointing at fallen trees. Others were using chainsaws, cutting the trees into more manageable pieces, but time was against them and it was getting darker by the minute. Peggy and Mr Flashman got out of the Jeep and walked over to one of the groups. 'This is Peggy Goody. She's offered to help us move the trees.' The men looked at each other and then at Peggy in total disbelief. 'Trust me,' said Jack Flashman. 'Let's get started.'

They went past the first tree that the men with the chainsaws were working on, and up to the next. Peggy said, 'Where do you want it moved to, Mr Flashman?' 'If you can lift it from underneath and push it over and away from the power lines my men will do the rest,' he instructed. Peggy positioned herself under the tree and said 'UP-UP' and as she reached the tree trunk with her outstretched hands the tree moaned and started to move upward. Peggy concentrated like never before. She knew if the tree should slip and fall back onto the power lines it would cause more damage and make the situation worse. Higher and higher she went until all the massive branches were clear, and then she gave one final push and over went the tree, away from the power lines. The men cheered and clapped, but she knew it was getting darker and there were four more trees to be moved.

'Show me the next!' she shouted, and in no time at all it was sent crashing to the ground, away from the power lines. The next three followed in quick succession, and only then did Peggy rest.

Jack Flashman gave Peggy a hug and said, 'I can't say how thankful we all are. I've never seen anything, anywhere, that even comes close to what you've just done. From all of us here, thank you, Peggy.' They sat for a while, then Jack said, 'Come on, Peggy, let's get you home. Your mother will be glad to see you back safe and sound.' When they arrived at Peggy's house her mother was waiting for her outside. Rose gave a little cry and ran to her. She hugged her daughter tightly, as if she would never let her go. 'I'm so proud of you,' she said.

Jack Flashman had telephoned Peggy's mother before they had started back and told her what Peggy had done and how brave she was. 'I have got to get back to my men now,' said Jack, 'and get everything back to normal. The good news is that the hospital will be out of danger thanks to Peggy. I'll be in touch with you tomorrow and discuss payment for tonight's work.' He said goodbye, got into his Jeep and drove away.

Peggy looked at her mother and shrugged her shoulders. 'I don't want payment,' she said. 'What I want right now is a hot bath because those trees were really dirty, and I'm starving.' Later, Peggy sat at the kitchen table with her mother and ate dinner. They talked for a while and went to bed. 'What a day it had been,' thought Peggy. 'First of all the library and Page Booker. And then the power cables.' And she fell into a deep sleep.

Unknown to Peggy, all her day's endeavours had been closely monitored by the Golden Fairy Queen, and with great satisfaction. She watched as Peggy drifted off to sleep and turned away from the Pool of Wisdom with a smile on her face. What a good decision she had made giving Peggy more magical powers, because she now knew that with Peggy they were in safe hands.

Chapter 12

THE VAN AND JIMMY

Jack Flashman was a very happy man. Thanks to Peggy's help he had been able to restore his customer's electricity supplies very quickly. Most important of all was Stitchery General Hospital, which had been switched on to emergency supplies but was now back to normal. He still found it hard to believe what Peggy had done but he was there and saw it with his own eyes. He decided to find out all he could about Peggy and her mother. And through this he discovered how Peggy's father, George Goody, died trying to save someone else, at the time when Peggy was still a baby. He also found out how hard Rose Goody had worked, taking in washing and ironing to feed them both when eventually her money ran out.

Jack talked to the people in the village and asked them about the Goody family and found out how much they were loved and what a tough time Rose Goody had gone through. But Rose had never given up, and brought up her daughter to be a kind and loving girl and now, it seemed, the village hero.

He asked about Rose Goody's laundry business and found out she needed to start up a collection and delivery service but could not afford to buy a van or employ a driver. 'Well, you can now, thought,' Jack Flashman. Without Peggy realising, she had single handed saved the Zeta Power Corporation tens of thousands of pounds and an untold amount of goodwill with their customers.

Jack decided there and then on a plan of action. He would present Rose with a large van fitted inside with hanging wardrobes and anything else that she could possibly need to run the service, and it would have a sign: Rose Goody Laundry Services. He would also reward the Goody family with a cheque for ten thousand pounds, which should pay for a driver until she was earning enough to cover his costs with the extra business it would bring in.

Three days later everything was in place. The van was ready and it looked splendid. It was sparkling white with sky blue lettering that had been carefully written. Inside were the best fittings, and it was taxed and insured for a full year. Jack had thought of everything. All it needed now was to present it to Rose.

Rose was working in the laundry and Peggy had gone to school. She had loaded up the tumble drier with the first wash of the day, and was about to take a quick tea break when the door bell rang. 'Who can this be?' she thought, and when she opened the door was surprised to see Jack Flashman. 'Good morning, Jack,' she said. 'What a pleasant surprise. Do come in. I was just about to have a tea break. Would you like a cup?'

'Thank you, that would be very nice,' he said, and sat down at the table.

'I hope you haven't had any more trees fall down,' said Rose, with a smile on her face.

'Goodness me, I hope not,' he said, returning the smile. 'No, Rose, I've come on a much more pleasant matter. First, I want to apologise for not contacting you last week, but I have been rather busy getting everything back to normal, and I've also been working out how to reward you and your daughter for getting both my company and me out of a very tough position.'

'Peggy didn't help you for gain. She helped you because she could. That's all there is to it,' said Rose.

Jack held up his hand. 'I know how you both feel, and that makes what I have to say even more pleasant. I've taken the liberty of helping you move your laundry business a stage further. It came to my attention that you needed to start a pick up and delivery service, but aren't able to fund it at the present time. You're probably not aware that the action you and your daughter took last week not only saved a great deal of time and chaos, but many thousands of pounds in man hours and equipment. And because of this, outside I have a surprise waiting for you. It's a laundry van with what I hope will be all the space that you'll need. It's taxed and insured for a year, and registered in your name as the owner. I also would like to give you a sum of money to fund a driver for six months or so.'

Rose stood up from the table with a shocked look on her face. 'I don't know what to say,' she said, a little shakily. She opened the envelope Jack handed her and when she saw it was a cheque made out to her for ten thousand pounds, sat back down with a thump. Her legs had turned to jelly. 'I've never seen so much money all in one place at the same time,' she stammered.

'Please say that you will accept our gift,' said Jack. 'Now come outside and look at the van, and tell me what you think.' Rose stood up again and went to the door, and as she walked outside the van was there right in front of her. It was not just a van, it was a large van, and top of the range with all the extras. She touched her name, written in sky blue on the side, tears of joy were running down her face. Rose had never dreamed that some day she would own something so beautiful. 'I don't know what to say,' she stammered. 'Oh, thank you, thank you so very much!'

Jack handed Rose the keys to the van. 'I'm sorry, Rose, but I do have to dash. Please go and have a sit inside and enjoy the moment.' He gave her a hug and kissed her on the cheek. Jack said goodbye, got into his Jeep, and left. As he drove away he had a warm feeling, that wonderful feeling when you know you have just done something right.

Back in Ireland the Golden Fairy Queen was looking into the Pool of Wisdom. She was watching Jack Flashman presenting Rose Goody with the van and the money she would need to employ a driver. How proud she was of Peggy. Even after such a long day, as soon as Jack Flashman had turned up on their door step asking for help Peggy had put her coat back on, and was ready to do anything that she was asked of her to help. She knew then that Peggy was destined to do many brave and wonderful things.

When Peggy arrived home from school she saw the van parked outside the house and thought they had visitors, but as she got closer she could see the name on the side of the van, Rose Goody Laundry Services. She rubbed her eyes and looked again, and as she did her mother came running towards her, shouting, 'It's ours—It's ours, Peggy!'

She flung her arms around Peggy and was jumping up and down with excitement. 'Come in the house and I'll tell you all about what has happened.' They both sat at the table and Peggy's mother went over all of Jack's visit. 'Tomorrow I'll have put the cheque in the bank, and now we have to find someone to do the driving for us.'

'I have an idea,' said Peggy thoughtfully. 'How about giving the job to Jim Smiley?'

Jim Smiley was a nice young man, nineteen years old and a hard worker, and had worked on Oak Farm since leaving school. But one day, about six months ago, he had a terrible accident, and after a long stay in hospital and several operations, came home with a very bad limp and a badly injured arm. He was no longer able to do farm work, and managed to stay positive, but he had not been able to find another job. Peggy said, 'I know he's got a driving licence—he got it when he worked on the farm so he could drive the tractor. Can we go and ask him? Maybe we can share our good luck with someone who needs some too.'

'What a thoughtful girl you are, Peggy,' said her mother. 'Come on, we'll both go and ask him right now.' Peggy knew were he lived because his sister Jenny was in her class and they were good friends. When they knocked on the door Jenny opened it.

'Hi, Peggy,' she said, surprised. 'Hello, Mrs Goody, please come in.' They went to the kitchen and sitting at the table were Mr and Mrs Smiley and Jim. 'I hope we haven't come at a bad time,' said Rose. 'No, of course not,' said Mrs Smiley. 'We've just finished our meal. Would you like a cup of tea?'

'Thank you. I suppose you're wondering why we've come out of the blue, so I'll come straight to the point. We've had some good fortune, and hope we might share it with you.' Rose quickly told them the story.

'So Peggy suggested we offer Jim the job of driving the van and organising the collection and delivery side of the business.' Turning to Jim, she said, 'What do you think?' Jim looked shocked. 'You know all about my accident. I'm over it now, but when I've been for other jobs they worry I won't be able to carry out the work load. I want you to know that if you take me on I would never let you down.'

'Well then, I've only got one question to ask you,' said Rose. 'When can you start?'

'Will tomorrow be good enough?' asked Jim.

'That would be great,' said Rose.

Jim stood up and shouted 'Yes!' and punched the air. It was the chance he had been waiting for. Rose shook Jim's hand. 'That's a deal, then.' Peggy was hugging Jenny because she knew what it meant to her and how much she loved her brother. On the way home Rose said to Peggy, 'You know, I think that is one of the best decisions we will ever make,' and squeezed her hand. They both smiled and carried on home.

Chapter 13

A Bad Day at the Council Building

Furnusabal had been working on a devilish plan. He intended to start a fire in the Council Building in Stonechurch, and for some time he had been studying the various times the building would be at its busiest. He had been sending his Imps into the building each night under the cover of darkness, and they had made plans for the fire alarm system and the sprinkler system, how to disarm them in a matter of seconds, and they had also found a way to stop the three lifts that ran up through the centre of the structure.

The building was only five years old and was fitted with the latest equipment. It was thirty storeys high, and as the first high-rise building in the town, was the council's pride and joy. Furnusabal's plan was to course an electrical fire on the fifteenth floor, and then disable the water sprinkler system, jam the lifts and stop the fire alarm from sounding, trapping the maximum number of unsuspecting people in the upper half of the building.

As he looked at his plans he could not contain his evil pleasure. 'It's pure genius!' he cried at the top of his voice, his ugly face contorting into a frightening grin, and shining bright red from the glow of the Fire Pit. 'Five hundred souls! I'll steal five hundred souls for my beloved Fire Pit. It will make me strong again.' His band of Fire Imps looked up at him as they danced around the Fire Pit, chanting, 'Master, master!' and clawing at the air with their wicked looking pointed fingers. Furnusabal sat back on his black granite throne 'Tomorrow,' he hissed, 'tomorrow.'

It was a normal day at the Council Building, with people rushing along attending to their business. But at 11.00 am all hell let loose. A fire started in a store room and spread into the main offices. The water sprinklers would not switch on and the fire was taking hold at an alarming rate. There was panic and everyone raced to the lifts but they were out of order, then ran to the emergency exit stairs. But coming up to meet them was a cloud of thick black smoke the Fire Imps were creating. The only way was up. Furnusabal's plan was going like clockwork.

Because the fire alarm had not sounded, the fire had a head start on the Fire Brigade, and it was going to be a tough one for them. Fortunately, the staff had been well trained and sprang into action. Office managers were shouting out orders to close and secure all fire doors and close the fireproof window blinds, this hopefully would slow down the fire spreading up the building, and give them all a chance to get to the higher floors. On the floors from underneath the fire, people were pouring out of the building and onto the street. The police moved them away from the building as quickly as they could, but in the panic they blocked the street and stopped the engines reaching the fire, and it was getting worse.

The Fire Brigade was soon in full swing down on the ground: five engines were in action, with all hoses trained on the building, and the extension ladders were up with hoses pouring water onto the blaze. But the fire was already burning on three floors now and spreading at a terrifying speed. On the ground the Chief Fire Officer was on the phone to general headquarters in neighbouring Grantal City. 'The fire looks like it's out of control, and as far as we can tell there are in excess of five hundred people trapped in the upper floors. We'll need helicopters to evacuate them from the roof, and any other assistance you can give us.' 'Leave it with me,' came the reply. 'We'll get there as soon as possible.'

The Chief Fire Officer's next call was to Sergeant Charger in Little Thatch. 'Charger, this is Chief Fire Officer Douser. We're in big trouble here. The Council Building is on fire and we have half the people in the building trapped on the upper floors. I want everything you've got that can help us, and can you get Peggy Goody over here as quickly as possible?'

'As good as done!' answered Sergeant Charger, and slammed the phone down. 'Listen up, lads. We've got big trouble in Stonechurch. The Council Building is on fire in a big way. They need all the help we can give them. Jenkins, take the car and go pick up Peggy Goody from school and bring her back here as quickly as you can. I'll talk to the Fire Chief, and we'll get over to Stonechurch.'

Jenkins drove off immediately and reached Saint Ann's school in record time. He dashed in and knocked on the Headmistress' door. 'Come in,' called Mrs Penn. P.C. Jenkins told her what was happening at the Council Building, and said that he had been asked to escort Peggy Goody over there to help them. 'Wait here,' said Mrs Penn. 'I'll go and get her for you. We don't want any unnecessary fuss do we?' She came back with Peggy, who already had her coat on and was ready to go. 'Don't worry about informing Peggy's mother,' said P.C Jenkins, 'Sergeant Charger is doing it.' 'Very well,' said Mrs Penn. 'Good luck, Peggy.'

As soon as P.C Jenkins returned to the station Sergeant Charger jumped into the car. 'Get the alarm going and don't spare the horses!' he shouted. 'Sorry to pull you out of school like this, Peggy,' and told her what was happening in Stonechurch. Peggy gazed out of the car window, thinking of when little Billy Stamp was trapped in the post office. That had been the work of Furnusabal and his band of Fire Imps. They had tried to kill him and steal his soul to cast into the Fire Pit. But this time it was much more serious. If Furnusabal was behind this, then a great battle lay ahead.

When they arrived at the Council Building the fire was burning on four floors. Because of the quick thinking of the staff in closing all the fire doors and window blinds, they had managed to slow down the spread of the flames, but it would not last long. The Chief Fire Officer stood by a table set up so he and the architect who had designed the building could try to find a way to contain the fire and, hopefully, put it out. The helicopters had arrived, but the news was not good. They had tried to get close enough and let down the harnesses to rescue people from the roof, but because of the updraft from the fire they could not risk going in close, and could only circle above on standby.

The architect had come up with a plan of action; it was very complex and would require precision timing. 'There's a two hundred and fifty thousand gallon water tank on the roof of the building, put there to pressurise the sprinkler system in case it failed. Obviously, something must have stopped it operating. If we can somehow puncture the roof in several places, and then set a charge directly underneath the water tank to blow at a given signal, and if we could co-ordinate the opening of all the fire doors at the same time, then we could blow the tank and flood the building. It just might put the fire out. Can we get someone on the roof? That's the question,' said the architect.

The Chief Fire Officer grinned. 'We've got a secret weapon,' he said. 'Leave it to me.'

All the time he had been keeping in contact with the managers in the building, he was now laying out his strategies with them. First, there would be eight sets of fireproof suits and visor helmets dropped onto the roof. These were for the volunteers who would open the fire doors on a given signal. They would have two minutes to get back up to their positions two levels up and secure themselves. In the meantime, all personnel must evacuate the roof and get to safety at least five floors down. One minute later the water tank would be blown and water would flood the building. Timing would be crucial. After going over it twice and making sure they completely understood, he signed off.

It was Peggy's turn to be briefed. 'Peggy, I want you to go up in the helicopter with our explosives expert. He'll lay six charges in strategic places on the roof to blast holes for the water to run through into the building, and a seventh directly onto the bottom of the water tank. We can't get close enough to the roof to lower him down. We need you to make yourself tall and place him on the roof. I must stress to you that it will be extremely dangerous.' But Peggy did not hesitate. 'OK,' she said, 'let's do it.'

They hovered over the rooftop but the helicopter was buffeted in all directions. 'This is as good as it gets,' said the pilot. 'Good luck.' Peggy was strapped to a man carrying a large holdall. 'Are you the explosive expert?' she asked. 'Yes,' he said. 'Are you sure you'll be able to hold me?' he asked, in a suspicious voice.

'Trust me,' said Peggy, 'we'll be alright.' They both sat on the side of the open helicopter door, and Peggy said 'UP-UP.' Her legs grew, and she readied herself to put her feet on the roof below. This was not going to be easy. The helicopter swayed violently and Peggy could not see where to step. Now that she had grown she picked up the man and jumped. She landed on the roof and immediately said 'DOWN-DOWN.' But as soon as they landed Peggy could see them—hundreds of Fire Imps, their bright red eyes glowing. They must have been there all night. And as soon as the Fire Imps saw Peggy they started to make their horrible thick smoke, and they started to choke. 'Blue Flash Help!' cried Peggy. In seconds a strong wind started to blow, and the smoke was being whisked away. But Peggy had to hang onto the man and guide him to the places that he indicated to her. The Fire Imps were defiant. They stood in Peggy's path, but she just brushed them aside but still they kept coming and so did the smoke. They were not going to give up without a fight. Peggy told the man to hold on to a steel bracket protruding from the water tank and she let go of him. She spun around to face the Fire Imps. They had lined up against her, but Peggy moved forward and began to lash out with her feet. She kicked and kicked and slowly they disappeared from the roof. When they were all gone, the man began to set the six charges on the roof and fixed the one on the water tank. Suddenly Peggy saw ten Fire Imps back on the roof going towards the charges. She was across the roof after them and had dispatched them into space in no time at all. The problem now would be getting back to the helicopter and blowing the charges before the Fire Imps could render them useless. Peggy waited until they were directly under the helicopter and screamed 'UP-UP!' They shot up and crashed into the open doorway. 'DOWN-DOWN!' she cried, and her legs came up to her. 'Blow them now!' Peggy shouted. She could see the Fire Imps swarming onto the roof. The man pressed the switch, and six loud bangs went off. Fire Imps were thrown into the air in all directions. The man pressed a second button and, as they looked down, they could see the water tank split down the middle and water gush through the holes in the roof. Their job was over and done. They peeled away from the building and prepared to land.

But inside the building it was panic. People clung onto anything they could as water poured through in a fierce torrent carrying all before it. Outside, all they could do was watch and pray. The water first passed through the top floor and great billows of steam shot out of broken windows. Then the next and the next—six floors in all. The crowd below stood, waited, and prayed. No one moved, and everything seemed to be in slow motion. Then came a shout, 'It's out, it's out!' The plan had worked.

The Chief Fire Officer was hugging the architect and jumping up and down. 'We made it, we made it! Now we can start to clean up and look at the damage.' As soon as the water had subsided enough the fire crews started to move in. It was thirty minutes before the first survivors came out; ambulances were waiting ready to give them treatment, and take them to hospital if need be.

Peggy had landed and was on her way back to the fire scene, and as she arrived the Chief Fire Officer moved towards her and held out his hands. 'Well done, Peggy,' he said, 'well done.' Peggy looked at him. 'Will you do something for me?' 'Yes, of course I will, anything. What would you like me to do?'

'I would like you to take me back to school and make no mention of me in connection with the fire today.' 'Why?' he asked. 'Without you hundreds of people would have died, you are a hero.' 'Sir,' Peggy said, 'there were things that happened on the roof of the building today that cannot be explained, and I don't want to be in the news.'

The Fire Officer nodded, 'If that is your wish, then I'll do all in my power to keep your name out of this, although I don't think it will be a total secret to everyone.'

Peggy was taken back to school and carried on as if nothing had happened. When she returned home in the afternoon she sat down with her mother and told her the whole story, and left nothing out.

The next day there was tragic news. Fourteen people had perished in the fire. It was late at night when the last of the bodies was brought out of the building, and by then everyone had been accounted for. Five hundred and seven had survived, and it was hailed as a small miracle. But even, so it had a hollow sound to it; Stonechurch was a town in mourning.

Peggy found out about the deaths when she got to school the next day. Everyone was in shock at the news; the children sat quietly at their desks while the headmistress explained to them what had happened. When she finished the headmistress announced that school would closed for the rest of the week, in respect for those who had died in the fire. Peggy and Cindy walked home together without saying much to each other, and as they parted Cindy said she would call Peggy later. When Peggy got home she told her mother what had happened at school, then buried her head in her mother's arms and sobbed uncontrollably.

In the forest Furnusabal had added another fourteen unfortunate souls to his pit. It had made him feel stronger, but it wasn't enough for the murdering beast. 'That interfering Goody again,' he said, talking to Demodus. 'Without her I could have had five hundred or more souls. My plan was working out perfectly until she showed up.' 'How did she know about the fire?' Demodus asked. 'The police went and picked her up from school and took her to the fire,' he answered, 'and between them they worked out a plan that stopped the fire. But they couldn't have done it without Goody and fairy magic.'

They looked at each other and agreed that the only way they would ever get their magic power back would be to kill Goody. They both went quiet and gazed into the air, contemplating the thought of seeing Goody dead.

Furnusabal was thinking to himself, 'If only I could steal Goody's soul and feed it into the Fire Pit, then all her fairy magic would be transferred to me.' He breathed out a long, loud evil hissing sound, and a smell of sulphur and smoke filled the air.

Demodus was thinking to himself, 'If only I could capture Goody and take her deep down into the mine, then I could slowly gain all the fairy magic from her body.' He looked over at Furnusabal. He had to be careful. Furnusabal could get inside his head and possibly read his thoughts. He may be my friend, but he had no doubt he would turn into his enemy to get what he wanted.

Chapter 14

THE JUBILEE RUN

The Daily News had four pages carrying the story of the fire at the Council Building; they were calling it 'Black Wednesday'. There was a picture gallery of those who lost their lives; it took up two whole pages and started with the youngest victims, Jill Prentice and Pam Long, two school leavers who had started working there only three months before. They were both bright young girls with their future prospects looking sound, but now sadly it was not to be. The list went on and on, the last one was Lilly Bradshaw. She had worked for the Council for twenty-eight years. She had a family of three children and seven grandchildren, and would be greatly missed, as would all those who perished in this awful tragedy. Peggy's hands were shaking as she read the story. She knew the true reason for the fire. It was that monster Furnusabal, with his insatiable thirst for death and destruction, and all aimed at stealing the souls of his poor unfortunate victims. She wondered just how much power he had gained from his victims, a more powerful Furnusabal was a terrifying thought

Unfortunately, the tragedy now seemed to be turning into a witch hunt. After all, none of the safety features in the building had worked, so someone had to be blamed, even though every system had been checked faithfully once every week and records had been made and filed with the Health and Safety Officer. Even a terrorist attack was not being ruled out. Peggy stared at the statement. 'If only they knew how close to the truth they were,' she thought, 'but the world would never know, because it is very hard to understand that which you cannot see.'

Peggy sighed and put the newspaper down on the kitchen table, and as she did her eyes wandered over to an article headed 'The Jubilee Run'. It was due to take place in two week's time, and would have ten railway carriages, all full of enthusiasts celebrating the age of steam. The train would be coming through Stonechurch, and would run through the railway station and on over the level crossing that ran through part of the town. 'That would be worth seeing,' she thought. 'I might ask Cindy to come and watch it with me.'

The telephone rang, and she crossed the room to pick it up. 'Hello, how can I help you?' she asked, thinking it was one of her mother's customers. 'This is Sergeant Charger,' said a gruff voice. 'Is this Peggy?' 'Yes,' said Peggy, surprised to hear his voice. 'Do you want me to get my mother?'

'No, it's you I want to speak to. Listen, Peggy, I need to ask you some questions about whet happened on Wednesday but I don't want to talk on the phone. If I send a car around for you, do you think you could spare me a little of your time down at the station?'

'Yes, of course. I'll go and tell my mother that you're coming to pick me up.'

'Thank you,' said Sergeant Charger. 'A car will be with you shortly,' and put the phone down.

Twenty minutes later Peggy walked into Sergeant Charger's office. 'Come in and sit down,' he said, smiling at Peggy. She chose a comfortable well worn brown leather chair and sat down. 'How can I help you, Sergeant?'

Sergeant Charger leaned across his desk, propping up on both elbows, his face cupped in his large hands. He gently rubbed his eyes, and when he removed his hands, his face looked strained and tired. Peggy knew the Sergeant had been on duty when the dead bodies were brought out of the Council Building, and it must have been a terrible experience for him. He looked over at Peggy. 'Were do I start? We called for your help because we know of your powers. It's no secret, we all know. What we don't know is what happened on the rooftop, and why did all the safety precautions in the building fail? There is so much we don't know. Is there anything at all you can tell me?'

Peggy thought for a while. 'I can tell you that the safety systems were disabled the night before the fire, and that the fire was started deliberately, but I don't know who it was.' Sergeant Charger looked stunned. 'Then what you are saying is that the victims were deliberately murdered.'

'Yes,' answered Peggy.

'When you were on the roof, with the explosive expert, what happened? In his report, he talks of a thick black smoke appearing on the roof from out of nowhere, and then after you had shouted something, a strong wind came and blew it away.

He also mentions that you seemed to be fighting something or someone while he was setting the explosive charges.'

'To a certain extent what he says is correct,' said Peggy, 'but I can't add anything to that. I can't speak of the things that are in my head or even write them down. I just can't. If you press me for answers I might have to relinquish my powers, then I won't be able to help you in the future. I know I've already failed fourteen people and I hate myself for letting them die, but I tried so hard. I promise you, Sergeant Charger, I did my best.'

'And your best was phenomenal,' said the Sergeant, holding Peggy's hand across the desk. 'Far from being a failure, you saved five hundred and seven people. And the irony is that no one will ever know it was you. The Chief Fire Officer told me of your wish to remain anonymous, and we will all respect this.' There was as moment of silence between them.

'Well, Peggy, I've taken up enough of your time. Thank you for coming to see me. I'll show you to the car and the driver will take you home. Please give your mother my best wishes and look after yourself.'

'Bye, Sergeant,' said Peggy, and off she went.

When Peggy arrived home Cindy was there. She was sitting chatting to her mother, and when she saw Peggy she jumped up and gave her a big hug. 'I'm so sorry,' she said. 'I didn't realise you'd been to Stonechurch at the fire. You didn't say anything about it when you got back to school.'

'I know,' said Peggy. 'It was awful. The screaming and crying for help, the heat and the smoke.' She looked at Cindy, her best friend. 'I can't tell you everything that happened but it was so bad.' Tears began to roll down Peggy's cheeks. It was a massive burden to put on the shoulders of one so young. She clung to Cindy, and the room went quiet.

Rose broke the silence. 'Time for tea and cake, I think,' she said, and the girls sat down at the table. It did the trick. All three of them started talking at the same time. They looked at each other and all burst out laughing. 'That's better,' said Rose. 'Now, Cindy, did you realise that in three weeks time it's Peggy's fourteenth birthday?' 'Yes,' said Cindy. 'And it's mine the day after.'

'That's interesting. Peggy's is on the Friday and yours is on the Saturday. I've been speaking to the school caretaker at your school about renting out the school hall for a party and he said that no one had booked it for that Saturday evening. He said we could book it until midnight, and has given me the telephone number of a disk jockey that plays at the school for a lot of the parties. We could do all the food ourselves.' 'You mean a joint party for Peggy and me?'

'Yes, that's the idea. Do you want to ask your mother?'

'Can I use your phone?' asked Cindy in an excited voice.

'It's by the window, help yourself,' said Rose.

Cindy came off the phone. 'Mother said I can, and she wants to talk to you, Mrs Goody, when you have the time.'

'I'll give her a call after dinner tonight,' she said. 'And now I must get on. The laundry won't do itself now will it?'

The Silver Fairy had been summoned to Ireland for a meeting with the Golden Fairy Queen. They were sitting together in the Operations Room, with Strake the Commander of Fairy Strategic Forces. This was the most secret of all the fairy operations, and was a well seasoned and lethal army unit. It was made up of the most powerful and magical fairies. Not only could they make themselves invisible, but they could also transfigure. They could move to most destinations in the world in seconds, with their specially adapted capsules, and through a network of underground tunnels using magic motion. They were issued with the most powerful military wands that could stun, kill or disintegrate depending on the situation, and they were in constant training and on high alert to tackle the threat of evil wherever it raised its ugly head.

The Queen began to speak. 'I have received some very disturbing news. As you are aware, for the last hundred years Furnusabal and Demodus have been helping each other in their many evil ventures, and despite their best endeavours we have managed to keep them in check for the best part, without too much effort. However eighteen months ago we had an incident where we had a fairy trapped and injured in the forest. She was Bluebell, the Silver Fairy's Chief Intelligence Officer. Her guise is that she looks after the flowers and plants in the forest, and this allows her to gather information without suspicion. She was trapped in the upper branches of a tree for quite some time and because she had not touched Mother Earth her energy was getting very low and she was unable to haze. Because of this a band of Demodoms spotted her and began sitting in the trees surrounding her, waiting for her to loose consciousness so they could capture her. Bluebell's only hope of escape was to do the unthinkable and involve a human, and she had no choice. The thought of the Demodoms taking her back to Demodus, who as we know would have attempted to drain her memory and all the fairy magic that she has; it could have been catastrophic for the fairy world.

'She could hear a young girl singing in the meadow next to the forest and was able to entice her into the forest and help her in her escape. Her name is Peggy Goody, who will be fourteen years old in three weeks time. She is a very brave and intelligent girl, and we have given her certain magic powers that she has used with remarkable success against both Demodus and Furnusabal, and in other good causes. Unfortunately, because she stopped both of them achieving their evil plans, she has angered both of them, and they have started to get much more adventurous in the human world. Without Peggy Goody, there would have been a great loss of human lives.'

She turned to the Commander and said, 'You, more than anyone, Strake, must remember the misery and suffering that Furnusabal's mother, Jesabal, created during the Great War. She was responsible for thousands of lives being lost, and stole thousands of souls for the Fire Pit in her volcano. And when you did manage to trap her in her volcano kingdom, it took your whole unit and all of their fire power to kill her, such was her power. And now it seems that sparing her baby son Furnusabal's life was probably a mistake, because he now seems to be following in his mother's footsteps, and that is very bad news.

'Now getting back to the information that I have received,' said the Queen, 'Demodus is reported to have captured Savajic Menglor, a dark wizard. If this is true, and he manages to drain out his memory and his magic, he will have a power equal to or even greater than Tiber the Gnome King. Savajic is no fool. He will have put several spells into place to stop such a thing happening, but we should never underestimate Demodus or what he may have in his underground kingdom. For over a hundred years he has been digging his many tunnels underneath stately homes stealing works of art and treasures. He has raided factories and laboratories and stolen scientific data. We cannot be sure of what he is capable of. I have informed King Tiber of the situation and he has promised to put his best fighters at your disposal should the need arise.'

'Thank you, your majesty,' said the commander. 'And if for some reason I should need Peggy Goody's help, can I rely on her?'

'Yes,' said the Queen, 'you can. Now we need a plan of action. We will meet back here tomorrow at noon.'

Peggy and Cindy had been busy inviting their friends to their party in the school hall, and it was going to be a great night. Sixteen boys and twenty girls were invited so far and there were more to come. The disc jockey was booked, and Peggy and Cindy's parents had organised the food and drinks. It was going to be great.

'What time are we meeting up on Sunday?' Cindy asked. 'The Jubilee Run is passing through at 3.15pm, so we need to be there at 2.45pm because I think there will be a crowd. Everybody is talking about it.'

Sunday arrived and it was a lovely sunny day, perfect weather for the Run, and Peggy was on her way to Cindy's house. Just as she arrived Cindy opened the door. 'I'm ready,' she said, 'let's get going.'

'I suppose Spencer Vincent will be there,' said Peggy. 'He might be,' said Cindy, blushing and giving out a silly giggle. Spencer was a prefect at the school and all the girls liked him. When he had been invited to the girls' party he had asked Cindy if he could be her partner for the night, to which she had said yes. And since then all the other girls had been teasing her. Peggy, on the other hand, had no trouble finding a partner. She had asked Jim Smiley. At first he was worried about his bad limp and his dancing, but Peggy would not take no for an answer, so he was going to pick up Peggy and her mother in the van and take them to the party, and when it was over he would take them back home.

The girls started walking toward the level crossing where the train would be passing by and as they got closer people were joining them from all directions. There was going to be quite a crowd, all cheering the train on its way. When they arrived the road was already closed off and there was a police car at each side of the crossing. The train was about ten minutes away and already the crowd had swelled to hundreds. Peggy and Cindy had a good position at the front. 'It's a good job we got here nice and early,' said Cindy, 'or we would have had trouble seeing it properly.'

A train whistle sounded in the distance. The train was coming. It blew again, and this time was much louder. The crowd strained forward to get a good look. Then the unthinkable happened. One of the police cars leapt forward and stopped right in the middle of the railway track. The policeman inside was frantically trying to start the engine but it would not turn over. The whistle blew again. This time it was only five hundred metres away and impossible to stop in such a short distance. There was going to be a terrible disaster. The crowd had nowhere to go as they were tightly packed together.

Peggy realised the police car was not going to move in time. She ran to the side of the car where the window was open, pushed both her arms in under the roof, spread her feet and screamed 'UP–UP!' She shot up into the air carrying the police car with her on her arms. The crowd ducked down fearing the worst. Peggy spread her legs wider just in time for the train to go through them. The train driver kept going but he was blinking his eyes. 'Had he really just driven through a pair of legs holding a police car up in the air?' he chuckled to himself, and said 'I think it's time I changed my specs.'

As the train disappeared in the distance, Peggy came back down to the ground with the police car. The crowd erupted, cheering and shouting her name. Peggy opened the car door and the when the policeman got out he fell to the ground, unable to stand, and was shaking and crying. The other policemen picked him up and took him over to the other car. Peggy moved quickly. 'Come on, Cindy, let's get away from here as fast as we can.' Cindy looked startled and followed her away from the crowd. They stopped and sat down on a bench by the church. 'What happened?' Cindy asked. Peggy looked at her. 'I'm not sure,' she said, 'but there could have been a lot of people killed here today and we were right in the front of it.'

Furnusabal was beside himself with rage. Another master plan lay in ruins because of that interfering Goody. 'What have I got to do?' he roared. Black smoke was pouring out of his hideous mouth and nostrils, and the Fire Imps were cowering in fear of their master. Two whole weeks finding out which policemen would be on duty at the level crossing, then getting into the mind of one of them, and making him drive onto the railway line just as the train arrived.

'All the souls that I could have stolen!' he stamped his big feet in rage, sending clouds of dust in the air and covering some of the Fire Imps. 'And to think of the power that I could have gained from it all he snarled. Then along comes Goody and snatches them away from me once again!'

But then as he settled down, an evil grin spread across his ugly face. He had kept his plan for the crash at the railway crossing quiet holding his cards close to his chest. It had been a secret. After all, why should he share it with Demodus? On the other hand, there was no secret that Goody and her friend were having a birthday party in the school hall next Saturday night. And this time he was sharing the plan with Demodus. The Demodoms were going to dig a tunnel leading directly under the school hall, and the Fire Imps would set fire to the school and lock all the doors. Demodus was to collapse the floor into the tunnel and snatch as many people as he could and take them back to his mine. And the ones that perished in the fire, he would steal their souls and feed them into the Fire Pit. He gave out a horrible blood curdling laugh. 'Next week, Goody, you'll burn as good as the next one, and then your magic will be mine, all mine!'

Chapter 15

THE BIRTHDAY PARTY

The Golden Fairy Queen, the Silver Fairy and Commander Strake, were deep in conversation. Spread out before them on a large table was a map showing the entrance to Demodus' mine, the gateway to his secret kingdom, and over on the right side of the map was the cave and Fire Pit of Furnusabal. 'Can we be absolutely sure that our intelligence information is correct, Commander?' The Queen was concerned about the timing of the operation they were about to mount. If it was not to the second things could go horribly wrong. Commander Strake had organised a reconnaissance squad of six out in the field, three at the mine and three at the Fire Pit, each one hazing and keeping a one hour watch. They listened and recorded every word that was said. The squad keeping watch on the mine had hit the jackpot. Furnusabal had been there to see Demodus to go over their plan to attack the school, and because the fairies left no scent they were able to get in close and record every word.

The plan was perfect for both of them: Demodus was only interested in the living, and Furnusabal wanted as many dead as possible. It was souls he was after. The plan seemed simple enough. Demodus would tunnel directly underneath the school hall, and at precisely 10 pm, when the party was in full swing, Demodus would collapse the floor. At exactly the same time the Fire Imps would set fire to the school and create a thick choking smoke to confuse everyone. It was up to Demodus to snatch as many people as he could before they were overcome. The remainder belonged to Furnusabal. They were both drinking wine and toasting their diabolical plan, and got drunker and louder.

'And so we have the time and the date,' said the Commander, 'but we are not taking anything for granted. Our squads are to stay in position just in case they have any last minute adjustments and change their plan.'

The Commander spoke again. 'My plan is to stop them before they can act. We start by burrowing our own tunnel to within one metre of the tunnel Demodus will be using, and thirty metres from the school end of their tunnel. At precisely twenty seconds before 10 we'll burrow through to their tunnel trapping the Demodoms at the school end of the tunnel and leave them with no escape route. If we're lucky Demodus will be there, too, but we're not expecting him to be, because his normal pattern is to stay back from the action and avoid capture.

'Because we have so little time to complete this action our wands will be set to destruct. There will be no evidence left to show that a battle has taken place and there will be no survivors. The second part of the plan is to have a team of six on the roof hazing; they will be watching the Fire Imps and they will attack in tandem with the tunnel squad. Before they can make their move to set fire to the school, we move in and blast them. Again, our wands will be set on destruct and, again, there will be no evidence that a battle has taken place.

'I do not think informing Miss Goody of our plan would be a good idea, because if she is looking at all preoccupied, the Imps or the Demodoms may just pick up on it and change their plan right at the very last minute. We cannot afford to let that happen. The whole plan relies on total surprise. We need to move in fast and hit them hard. I believe that it is the only way to do it if we do not want the humans to be involved. Then after we have cleaned up, I intend to leave the team up on the roof, in case they plan a return visit, which I very much doubt, but just to be on the safe side.'

The Commander paused and said, 'Your Majesty, this is my plan, and I ask for your approval'.

The Queen looked over to the Silver Fairy and said, 'This battle will be fought in your territory. It has my approval but I also feel you should have the last word on the plan.'

The Silver Fairy nodded. 'Your Majesty, both Demodus and Furnusabal have been behaving very badly towards the humans and they are getting worse by the day. I know that we have probably upset them by giving Peggy Goody magical powers, but I think this plan will teach them a sharp lesson that it is not just Peggy Goody they have to deal with in their evil ways. The plan has my full support, Your Majesty.'

The Queen turned to Commander Strake and said, 'Draw up your battle plans and may good fortune go with you.'

The Commander bowed to the Queen, thanked her and left. She could not wait to get started.

It was Friday afternoon, and while Peggy and Cindy packed their books and things away in their school bags, they chatted with great excitement. 'Tomorrow night!' said Cindy, 'I can't wait. Spencer Vincent is actually coming to my house to pick me up and take me to the party. I can't believe it.' 'Why not?' said Peggy. 'You're the prettiest girl in the school. It's Spencer who should be honoured that you said yes to him.' Cindy was blushing. 'Do you really think that?' 'Yes, I do,' said Peggy, 'because it's true, and don't forget all the dance practice that we've been doing for the last three weeks. Trust me, Spencer Vincent is in for a big surprise.'

When Peggy arrived home she hung her school bag on the door and went to see her mother in the laundry. She saw Peggy and looked up from her work. 'Hi, I'm home. Would you like me to bring you a cup of tea?' asked Peggy. 'Yes, please,' she answered. 'This is the last load today, so will you leave my tea on the table please? I'll be just a couple of minutes.' And by the time Peggy had made the tea, her mother was sitting at the kitchen table. 'How was your day at school?' she asked. Peggy shrugged her shoulders. 'OK, I guess,' she answered.

Her mother looked at her surprised. 'That's not like you, dear. Whatever is the matter? Are you feeling poorly?' 'No, I'm alright. It's just that it's our party tomorrow night, and Cindy has been going on all day about the new dress her father bought her. I'm not jealous, honestly, I'm not, and I love you more than anyone in the world. But sometimes I wish I had a father as well, to look after us.'

'I have that wish too,' said Rose, 'but it's not to be for us. But I will say this to you. If it is possible, tomorrow night he will be looking down, proudly watching his beautiful daughter having a good time with all her friends and wishing he could be there, too, holding you in his arms, and taking you on to the dance floor for the first dance.'

'Now, then,' she said, changing the subject, 'about your new dress. Tomorrow afternoon we will be shopping in Stonechurch, for a dress, and shoes and a jacket, and I think it is about time you tried on some high heels. And if that doesn't knock them all dead at the party, then nothing will.'

Peggy beamed with excitement. 'I can't wait, I can't wait,' she cried. 'Can I choose anything I like?' Her mother laughed and said, 'Yes, as long as you don't break the bank.'

Peggy woke up and rubbed her eyes. 'Saturday at last!' she thought. She jumped out of bed and looked out of the window. Outside she could see her mother helping Jim Smiley load up all the weekend deliveries. It was an early start today because they wanted to be finished by lunch time, to give them plenty of time to get ready for the party and, of course, Peggy's shopping spree.

Commander Strake had assembled the soldiers together. They were in the process of checking their equipment: they wore special lightweight jackets and helmets to give them protection and allow them to fly freely. The helmet was state of the art, with the latest communications system known as WISPER—wide inner spectrum penetration ear receptor. It had been developed specifically for underground communications and the fairy laboratories had devised a way to bring together very high frequencies with very low frequencies in a revolving helix, and the result was staggering. It could penetrate through one metre of solid lead. The visor had the latest night sight and heat-seeking vision, making it possible to see in almost any conditions, and was also fitted with FAG—Fresh Air Gill, a breathing device that would give up to twenty-four hours of normal breathing, even in the densest and most poisonous smoke fumes. In the top of the helmet was Hawk Eye a device that recorded everything the wearer saw through the visor and was played back in the form of a three dimensional hologram. The wand fitting was also a very important part of their preparation: each wand had its own signature, and only the fairy that carried it was able to use it and make it fire. It was the only wand in the fairy world that was fitted with a pistol gip and fired with a trigger. The laser that it fired was powerful enough to disintegrate any known material, and should it be lost in battle it would be useless to anyone else. After all the equipment had been sorted and issued, Commander Strake called her force together for a preparation meeting in the operations room. 'I want to make this clear from the off. This is not an easy operation. The tunnel squad will be fighting in a very confined space, and as you have found out today, our wands will be set to destruct. Your enemy are the Demodoms. They are not natural fighters but extremely agile and have very strong arms and claw-like hands. We estimate there will be at least thirty of them in their tunnel; our job is to kill them off as quickly as possible and to leave no trace that a battle has taken place. When you have completed your mission you will seal both tunnels and retreat back to the Silver Cave in the forest.

'The roof squad will have the advantage of being able to fly but, again, not an easy task. The Fire Imps are very illusive and can easily hide in small dark places and they can also jump very high and at speed. They also have the ability to create thick black smoke as a camouflage. Your shooting skills will be tested as never before. You must eliminate them all. Your task is to stay on the roof until the party is over and all the humans have left for home. They must be kept safe, and have absolutely no idea that a battle has taken place. Then when you are sure of success, fly back to the Silver Cave. Both squads will at all times be in full haze and, remember, your wands will be set on destruct, so be careful out there. Are there any questions? No? Then you are dismissed.'

Deep in the forest, a different scenario altogether was being played out. 'Is the tunnel complete?' asked Furnusabal. 'Yes,' said Demodus. 'If we move out at 9.30 pm it will give us plenty of time to get everything in place, and we will also have the cover of darkness to our advantage.' 'Excellent!' roared Furnusabal. 'I will go now and make sure my Fire Imps know our part of the plan back to front. I will be back here at 9.30 pm precisely.'

Demodus watched him go, his ugly mouth curled as he gave a menacing grin. 'You fool,' he mumbled. 'I am fully aware of your plan to capture Goody's soul for yourself, but you are nowhere near clever enough.' Demodus had recently raided a communications factory and had made off with the very latest hi-tech listening devices, and he had also captured one of the technicians and taken him back to his underground kingdom. Once there he had forced him to teach his Demodoms and himself how it all worked. And since then, unknown to Furnusabal, he had surrounded his cave and the Fire Pit with the most sophisticated listening devices in the world. He learned that Furnusabal had found out where the disc jockey for the party lived and while he slept put a suggestion into his mind. At precisely 9.57 pm he was to invite Peggy Goody and her friend, Cindy, to the centre of the dance floor so their friends could sing Happy Birthday to them. His Fire Imps would pinpoint

Goody, throw the main light switch, and in the dark pull her to the side of the building away from the hole the Demodoms were to make at precisely 10.00pm to snatch their prisoners.

As Demodus was talking to his Demodoms and changing the timing of his attack to suit the information he had received, the reconnaissance fairy was recording every detail. Commander Strake, in her wisdom, had been correct in leaving her squad in place right up until the last minute. There was no honour between these two monsters and neither one deserved any quarter from the fairy soldiers.

As Commander Strake received the news she gave a wry smile. She couldn't say she was totally surprised. After all, cheats rarely change their evil ways. Her briefing was short and to the point. 'We have a change to our operation tonight. Our attack will now begin at 9.50 pm precisely. We will hit them hard and fast. They must be stopped at all cost. We will need to be in position at 9.30 and in total silence. Good luck. Now rest up. Your fairy magic will need to be at its maximum power.'

It was 5.30 when Peggy and her mother arrived back home. What a fantastic time she had had. She had been into so many shops and tried on so many things, it was something she would never forget. 'Thank you, mother, it's the best day I've ever had.' And they hugged each other. At 7.30 Rose Goody was putting the finishing touches to her daughter's hair. She stood back and looked at her. It suddenly hit her that she was looking at a beautiful young lady. Peggy had wide bright green eyes and shiny golden hair, and she was tall and slim. She had chosen a green figure hugging dress that flared out at the bottom and green shoes with a small heel and a delicate white piping around the top, and to finish off, a short white jacket.

'Oh, Peggy, you look so grown up. I am really proud of you.'

'And I am really proud to have a mother like you,' replied Peggy.

There was a knock on the door. Peggy opened it and Jim Smiley was standing there. 'Wow!' he said when he saw her. 'You must be an older sister' and they both stood there laughing. 'Mrs Goody, your carriage awaits you,' said Jim, with a cheeky look on his face. Rose put on her coat and linked arms with Peggy. 'Come on, Peggy let's knock 'em dead.' They all got into the van and off they went, and Peggy felt like Cinderella going to the ball.

They arrived at the school hall at 7.50, just as Cindy was getting out of her father's car with Spencer Vincent. 'Hello, Cindy, hello Spencer,' she said. Cindy just looked at her without saying a word. 'Is something wrong?' asked Peggy. 'No,' said Cindy, 'you just look so different. It's the first time I've ever seen you in a dress. You look really great. Come on, let's go in.'

As they entered the school hall a big cheer met them. They had all been asked to arrive a little bit early to welcome the girls. The disc jockey began with a slow number and the party took off. Peggy grabbed Jim's hand and said 'Come on, Jim, just one for my birthday.' He could not dance very easily and Peggy knew it, but she held him close and swayed to the music. When the song finished they went back and sat down by her mother. Then when the music started again Peggy found herself in great demand, and the boys had suddenly noticed her. It was to be the start of a great night.

At 9.30 Commander Strake had both of her squads in place. The party inside was going well, the music was loud, and there was a lot of talking and laughing. On the roof the soldiers were hazing when, suddenly, the first of the Fire Imps appeared. They were climbing up the walls and within a few minutes the roof was swarming with what must have been a hundred of them. They were looking all over the roof making sure no one was about, their eyes burning red in the darkness of the night. They made a scratching noise with their clawed feet as they scampered across the slate roof of the school, the tension was almost unbearable. The roof squad hovered about five metres over them, waiting for the order to start blasting them out of existence. There would be no mercy shown, because they knew the Fire Imps would show no mercy to the innocent children below just wanting to have a good time; and they were more than happy to carry out Furnusabal's murderous plan and steal their souls.

Meanwhile, the tunnel squad were monitoring the Demodoms' movement in the tunnel. The Demodoms moved slowly toward the cave, directly underneath the school hall. The sound of their footsteps was eerie, and the tension in the tunnel was electric. The squad adjusted their helmets. When the order came they had to be ready to go. There were three wands pointing at the wall that separated the two tunnels and it would disappear at the first blast. The movement in the Demodom tunnel suddenly stopped. They were now in position and ready to attack. Both of Commander Strake's squads were poised and ready to strike.

They looked at their army issue digital wrist watches. The count down had started. 'Ten-nine . . . One-ero-GO-GO-GO!' The roof squad started blasting. The first twenty were easy pickings, but after the initial surprise the Fire Imps were on the move. They used the shadows to great effect and then came the smoke, a thick dense black choking fog that enveloped the whole roof. It was time for the squad to move in close. Their helmets would stop them from choking, but now the Fire Imps would only be seen as infra-red images and much more difficult to hit. 'Keep them from getting to the electrical mains!' ordered the Commander. 'They must not be allowed to throw the switch.' The Commander's voice was clear and crisp, with no sign of panic. Imp after Imp died trying to get to the box but they were repelled. Two of the squad stood back to back and blasted them away.

Then there came the call they all dreaded. We have a 'Soldier down—Soldier down.' The Imps had overwhelmed one of the squad and were trying to tear off her helmet. If they could steal a fairy soul with all its magic their master would be well pleased. The Golden Fairy Queen was following the battle closely in the Pool of Wisdom. She had given instructions to the Silver Fairy to send Bluebell to the battle and blow away the smoke from the school roof. Bluebell had summoned up the wind and the smoke was slowly clearing. The downed soldier came into view. Two of the squad went to her aid, blasting the Imps as they got closer. The soldier was soon back on her feet again and firing at the Imps. The army of Imps was getting smaller, but there was no sign of them giving up. Their fear of death was much less than having to face their master, Furnusabal, with failure.

The tunnel squad, on their 'Go-Go-Go' signal, had blasted through the rock separating the two tunnels and were fighting their way towards the cave under the school hall. They had taken the Demodoms completely by surprise, but unfortunately they were to discover they only knew half of Demodus' plan. He also had a back up plan, but they found out too late. Demodus was a Gnome, and Gnomes were renowned for their planning, battle skills, and bravery. The Commander had assumed all of the Demodoms would be lying in wait in the cave under the school hall, ready to snatch as many children as possible. This was, unfortunately, only half true. Demodus had a much more sophisticated plan. Yes, there were a large number of Demodoms in the cave, but the Commander did not know they were armed with gas cylinders containing a quick action gas that would render the children unconscious immediately. As they fell into the cave, it would be relatively easy to transport them back to his mines. Demodus wanted as many prisoners as possible, so he had formed a second team of Demodoms to wait further up the tunnel to transport the prisoners back to his mines and by doing so leave the Demodoms in the cave free to capture more children. Instead of concentrating all their fire power in the direction of the cave they had to fight a rearguard action as well. Fortunately their helmets protected them from the gas, but they struggled to keep them on. The squad had split to a formation of four to the front and two to the rear, all the time moving deeper into the cave. Six Demodoms were left, and they made a dash forward in an attempt to break through, and possibly tear the masks off the soldiers. The Demodoms hit the squad head on. Two were disintegrated instantly, but four Demodoms made it. They were grappling hand to hand now with their strong arms overpowering the soldiers and their claws slicing into the soldiers' flesh. Two of the soldiers managed to point and fire their wands, and the Demodoms disintegrated. Then they took aim at the other two Demodoms, fired, and they were gone, but they were too late. Both soldiers were dead. The Demodoms' claws had ripped across their throats, almost taking off their heads. The two soldiers turned and faced the other way, now they were a squad of four, their wands were firing like never before, and their rage was plain to see. The Demodoms realised all was lost and, without any chance of taking prisoners, turned and fled up the tunnel, back to the mines, but they were not pursued.

The soldiers' orders were to seal the tunnels and return back to the Silver Cave. One of the soldiers went back down into the cave and destroyed all the gas cylinders, then, using her wand, sealed up the tunnel behind her. They also sealed off their own tunnel and started back to the Silver Cave, carrying their two dead comrades.

On the roof the battle was nearing its end. Three soldiers had sustained wounds when the Fire Imps leapt into the air and managed to claw their legs. Finally, when the last of the Fire Imps had been dispatched and an inspection of the area carried out, to make sure there were no survivors hiding away, the squad landed on the roof. They were completely exhausted, but their orders now were to stay on the roof until the very last person had left the building and gone home. It was now 10.45 and the battle was over. The mission had been accomplished. The Commander decided not to tell the roof squad of the two deaths in the tunnel until they returned to the Silver Cave later. She issued orders to the soldiers for half of the squad to go down to the ground and recharge their energy and then change places with the other half of the squad—fairies used up a large amount of energy when they hazed.

At 9.57, exactly, Josh Spinum, the disc jockey, invited Peggy and Cindy onto the dance floor for everyone to sing Happy Birthday to them. He did not know why he was doing it at this time in the evening, because he had never done it before. The girls held hands in the middle of the dance floor and they all sang Happy Birthday to them at the top of their voices. They were totally unaware of the battles raging above and below them. But for the fairy soldiers and their sacrifices, the consequences would have been devastating. They would never know, not even Peggy. The party carried on and everyone was having a great time and then, like all good things, it came to an end. Josh Spinum said, 'Please take your partner for the last dance and, once again, a happy birthday to Cindy and Peggy, and I hope you all enjoyed the music' to which he had loud applause. 'Thank you, very much,' he said, and the last dance started. Half an hour later the school was deserted.

The Commander had assembled her squad and took off for the Silver Cave. But when they arrived the mood was solemn, and it did not take long to find out why. The two deaths were a bitter pill to swallow, but they were hardened professionals. Commander Strake had given the Silver Fairy the results of the mission and news of the unfortunate deaths of the two soldiers. She thanked her for sending Bluebell to aid them and dispel the smoke. 'And now I must return to the Queen,' said the Commander. 'Thank you once again.' The Commander and soldiers boarded their capsules and left for the Golden Cave.

The capsules came to rest quietly in the docking bay, and the Commander was the first to climb out. Two soldiers standing guard saluted her, and she returned the salute. Two stretchers were waiting for the dead soldiers and they were carefully laid on and covered over. Commander Strake stood between the two stretchers and laid her hands out, one on each body and bowed her head. She was the consummate professional, but to her this was personal. After a few moments, she lifted her head and said 'Carry on,' and walked away toward the Throne Room, where she knew the Queen would be waiting for her report. The soldiers carried their two dead comrades to the Golden Cave, where the Golden Birthing Tree stood. It was the order of things. There would be no mourning or burial. The soldiers' bodies would be undressed and laid to rest under the Golden Birthing Tree, where their seeds would sink into the ground and two young baby soldiers would be born. This was the way the fairy army stayed strong and resolute.

Chapter 16

SAVAJIC THE DARK WIZARD

Peggy woke up to the sound of birds singing outside her bedroom window, and lay in bed thinking about the party. It had been a great night and everyone had enjoyed themselves. She had danced with most of the boys there, and soon found out that boys were not all silly and could be really funny and fun to be with. She also noticed that Cindy and Spencer had been together all night, and she wondered how much longer Cindy and she would be doing everything together as best friends. Then her thoughts drifted back to the fire at the Council Building and how she had been asked for her help by Sergeant Charger. Was this going to be her future role in life, possibly working for the police? Who knows where her magic powers would lead her, she thought.

It was a different kind of Sunday morning at the mine of Demodus. Furnusabal had turned up unannounced and was screaming at Demodus at the top of his voice. 'You fool! You must have done something to alert the fairies. Have you any idea of the damage this has caused me? One hundred and ten of my Fire Imps were obliterated. The fairy soldiers were there waiting to ambush and slaughter them. They must have known of our plans in advance. I never told them so it must have been something you said or did.'

Demodus stood in front of Furnusabal and thrust his ugly face into his. 'Because you are very upset, I am going to forget that you have just called me a fool, but it will not happen a second time, believe me. Now sit down and listen.' His voice was menacing. Furnusabal went quiet and sat down.

'The fairies were also lying in wait for the Demodoms, and their timing was much too good to be a coincidence. They must have somehow seen our plans. My loss was twenty-three Demodoms. They are not trained fighters, but they still managed to kill two fairy soldiers with their claws. It's scant consolation for my losses, but at least it is something for me. But now back to our problem. I have given this much thought. Each time that we discussed our plan it was here, out in the open. Now just suppose that we were being watched and even now, as we speak. We both know that the fairies travel about invisibly. They could have even been looking over our shoulders, seeing and hearing everything that was said. From now on, any plans we make together will have to be made underground.'

And as he was saying it Demodus was thinking to himself, 'And that will be when your Fire Pit freezes over.' He did not trust Furnusabal the least little bit, and he would never let him see what he had in his underground kingdom. He rose slowly and said, 'Now, unless you have further business to discuss with me I would like to be left alone.' He turned and walked back into his mine. Furnusabal just stood there feeling very stupid indeed.

Demodus did not believe in dwelling in the past. What was done was done and gone. His priority now was to break Savajic the Dark Wizard. He needed his magical powers now more than ever to go up against the fairy world, and he knew that time was running out. Savajic had been locked in a dark cell, gagged, and tied to a heavy chair; his wand had been taken away from him and hidden in a safe place.

The door to Savajic's cell was flung open and in strode Demodus. 'Good morning, oh Dark One,' he leered at Savajic. 'Are you ready to release your secrets to me?' Savajic looked at him with his dark eyes, and thought, 'How could I have been so stupid to let this unspeakable creature capture me, is beyond belief.'

Savajic had used his magic powers to give himself a millionaire lifestyle. He lived in a stately home that had been left empty for some fifty years, and he had acquired it and all the surrounding land belonging to the estate. He had bought and paid for it through one of his human servants, whom he had mesmerised for the task. Unlike many of the Dark Wizards, he was fair and generous, and he looked after his servants very well indeed. The stately home had been renovated to a very high standard and it lacked for nothing, as did Savajic himself. He had converted the massive wine cellar into his magic workshop and it was while he was trying out a new spell that he had been caught off guard and allowed Demodus to capture him. Demodus was a natural thief; and he had been targeting stately homes ever since he had tunnelled underneath one by pure chance. He had broken through into one of the cellars and wandered around upstairs in the darkness looking at all the treasures in amazement. It was right there and then he got his appetite for the finer things in life. Since then he had searched the country robbing some of the finest houses, just the odd items from each, but there were many, and his total haul was huge. His great cave was something to behold, from works of art and furniture to carpets and statues from famous collections.

The Savajic robbery, however, was totally different to all the others. Demodus had located its position and broken into a small cellar next to the magic workshop. But as he looked around he realised that the owner was a wizard. He covered his tracks and went back to the mine, where he immediately started to work on a plan to capture the wizard. Sometime earlier he had tunnelled underneath a military store depot and stolen a number of gas canisters containing a fast acting sleeping gas. His plan was simple: he would take two sleeping-gas canisters with him and put them in the cellar next to Savajic's magic workshop, lay in wait until he was there concentrating on one of his spells, and then gently release the gas and render him unconscious.

When Savajic put his Exclusion Spell around his home it was powerful enough to ward off any living thing on earth, but he had not even considered the possibility of an intrusion from underground, and this had always been the ace card Demodus played, which made him such a successful thief. Demodus had been in position and waiting for some three hours in the cellar, but it did not matter how long it took because the prize was so great.

The door suddenly opened and Savajic walked into his magic workshop. He was completely unaware of Demodus, lying in wait in the next cellar, or of the hole that had been bored through the wall to let in the sleeping gas. He began work on his latest spell and was soon totally engrossed in what he was doing. Demodus slowly and carefully started the gas flowing through the hole in the wall. It was odourless and invisible and it started to creep around the room like an evil plague. Demodus was preparing the second canister. One would have been enough but he was not taking any chances. There was no need to rush or panic, the result was all that mattered. An evil grin had spread across his face. 'Soon you will be mine,' he whispered to himself.

In the next cellar Savajic was swaying. He was suddenly feeling very sleepy. He sat down and fell back into a deep sleep. Demodus appeared and went straight over to Savajic and prodded him with his claw. There was no response, but he knew he must move quickly. First, he searched for Savajic's wand, found it and tucked it safely into his belt. Then, with a roll of duck tape he had brought with him, bound his arms and legs and gagged him. He picked him up and made his way back to the mine. And now here he was, his prisoner. But how could he steal the magical powers that Savajic possessed? He had tried to drain his secrets directly from out of his head, but to no avail. He decided he would have to torture him, it was the only way. Savajic followed every move Demodus made, his eyes tracking the smallest inflection. Like Demodus, he could see in the dark, but he guessed Demodus thought he couldn't. Suddenly, his body arched in pain. A razor sharp claw slashed across his chest. Demodus growled, 'Now, let's see if that has loosened your tongue,' and ripped the gag from out of Savajic's mouth.

'Uncaptivus!' screamed Savajic. There was a blinding flash of bright orange light and Demodus was thrown violently across the cell and smashed into the wall. The chair splintered into a thousand pieces and Savajic had disappeared. Demodus had foolishly underestimated the magical powers Savajic possessed. He knew he should never have taken the gag from his mouth, but he thought that without his wand he could not cast a spell. Then it hit him! He still had Savajic's wand, hidden away and only he knew where it was, so perhaps all was not lost.

There was a bang and a puff of smoke, and Savajic reappeared in his magical workshop, bleeding from a deep gash across his chest. He crossed the room to a large glass cabinet, opened the door and took out a jar of green liquid. He poured some onto his hand, then smoothed it across his chest. It turned into a dark green mist that hung there for less than a minute, and when it had cleared away the gash had healed without leaving a trace.

He wasted no time cleaning and changing his clothes. There was a much more important matter to deal with. He immediately set about putting an Exclusion Spell deep into the ground, directly under his home, and when he had finished he sat back in his chair and rested. He knew Demodus still had his wand hidden away and it would be almost impossible to get it back without help of some kind. His wand was a great part of his magic powers and without it he would not be able to go into any kind of battle and expect to win. He knew he could get help from his fellow wizards if he asked, but he also knew it would lead to much ridicule from his peers. A wizard who had graduated from the Black Eagle School for Wizards, allowing a Gnome to capture him, and take him as his prisoner and steal his wand, it was unthinkable. Worse still, Savajic had a son, Owen. He was fourteen years old and a student at the Black Eagle School for Wizards—imagine his embarrassment. He decided to leave his magic workshop, have a meal, and relax. There was no need for panic. He would find a solution to his problem, and he just needed a little time to think it through.

After dinner Savajic sat quietly in his study. His plush well worn leather chair felt like an old friend with whom he could relax. His butler, Cooper, brought in a silver tray with a decanter of his favourite Germain-Robin Alambic brandy and a clipped Cuban cigar. 'Will there be anything else, sir?' Cooper asked. 'No thank you, Cooper. You can retire for the evening.' Cooper said good night and left the room, closing the door quietly behind him. Savajic lit his cigar, letting the smoke curl slowly into the air. He reached over to the decanter and poured himself a large brandy, and sipped it slowly. The smooth rich taste gave him a glow of well being, and he settled back in his chair and closed his eyes.

His thoughts drifted back into the past, and he saw his beautiful Megan wandering in the valley in Snowdonia National Park, where he had first seen her. She had been on a visit with friends, and he had been in his last month at Black Eagle School. The school was built into the side of a high mountain, completely invisible to the naked eye, and had a large balcony running the width of the building, from where the students could look down into the valley. It was a sunny summer's day and Savajic was looking down into the valley with the aid of his friend's binoculars, when he spotted Megan. Immediately he knew he must get to meet her, and eventually he did. And four years later they were married. The Council of Wizards frowned on mixed marriages and did not encourage them, but never the less Savajic managed to get their permission.

Two years later their son Owen was born. He was strong and healthy and had his mother's raven black hair. Savajic could see her now, holding little Owen and laughing. They were so happy and so in love. Owen was just four years old when Megan was struck down with a terrible disease, but despite all of the wizards' magic, they could not cure her and she died, at just twenty-seven years old. Savajic and Owen were shattered by her death and it took a very long time for them to come to terms with it, but they did and eventually Owen started his first year at The Black Eagle School for Wizards, while Savajic worked his magic in the London Stock Exchange where he amassed a large fortune.

The picture faded in his mind and suddenly he was back in the dark cell where he had been held prisoner by Demodus. His mood changed to irritation as he thought how easily he had been captured. Then again, he had at least had the foresight to have put a permanent Uncaptivus Spell on Owen and himself with a verbal command that would immediately bring them back to the magic workshop. He had worked on the spell and perfected it for such an occasion, and it had worked perfectly and so, at least, it gave him the satisfaction of outwitting the ugly Demodus.

'Now back to the problem of my wand,' he thought. 'I am going to need some help on this one.' Then he had an idea. When he was a young boy he had helped a fairy who had been netted in a trap set for catching birds by a notorious poacher called Ned Snerum. She had called out to him for help while he was in the forest collecting herbs and fungi for his father. When he found her she was badly tangled up in the net, and because she had struggled to get out it had got tighter and tighter until she could not move at all. He cut her loose and helped her get home, where he had been thanked for his help, and the fairies had promised help in return if he ever needed it, and if he ever did he was to close his eyes and say 'Blue Flash Help' and he would be contacted by an intelligence fairy called Bluebell. 'That may be the answer,' he thought, 'but not now, tomorrow.' He put his cigar down and took a final sip of brandy and then closed his eyes once more, this time drifting off into another world, a world that belonged to him with Megan at his side.

The next morning Savajic felt ready to make his contact. He looked into the mirror. 'It's now or never,' he said out loud to his reflection. He turned and said 'Blue Flash Help'. There was a flash of blue light and there, perched on a chair, was Bluebell. 'Good morning, Savajic. How are you today?'

'I am well,' he replied. 'It really is very good of you to come so quickly.'

'It is no trouble at all,' said Bluebell. 'We owe you a favour for rescuing Fern all those years ago, and we are flattered that you have asked us for your help. We were very concerned when we learned of your capture by Demodus.'

Savajic looked surprised. 'I was kind of hoping to keep it a secret,' he said, feeling a little foolish. 'How did you find out?'

'We have a network of intelligence that covers many lands, and we concentrate on what we call "Hot Spots". Demodus' mine is one such spot and we knew of your capture on the day it happened. We would have made an attempt to rescue you, but the fairy world is not allowed to enter another living creature's home or property unless it has permission or a magical connection to someone or something inside.'

'Then I am afraid I have wasted your time,' said Savajic, and went on to explain what had happened in the mine, and how he had escaped, but minus his wand.

'There may be a way,' said Bluebell, thoughtfully. 'A few years ago I found myself in a similar position to Fern at the time when you helped her all those years ago. I, too, was trapped in the top of a tree, badly injured and in danger of being captured by the Demodoms and taken prisoner. Fortunately, I was able to enlist the help of a young girl, Peggy Goody, who saved me from capture. We have always had an unwritten law that says we never make contact with the human race, but this time the consequences would have been too grave to contemplate. For the bravery she showed, our Queen has given her magical powers and she has used them to save hundreds of lives. She is joined to us by fairy magic and this may be the answer. Wherever she goes I can follow. I would obviously have to get both the Queen and Peggy to agree to go along with any plan we might come up with, but I am sure it is possible.'

Savajic looked at Bluebell and said, 'I, too, broke the rules. I fell in love and married a human. After much deliberation The Council of Wizards gave their permission for a mixed marriage to take place and I married my Megan. Two years later we had a son, Owen, who is now in his fifth year at the Black Eagle School for Wizards. So, as you see, I have a close relationship with humans, and I would welcome the chance to meet Peggy.'

Bluebell stood up. 'I will do my best to help you. I will see the Queen and find out how we can get your wand back, but now I must go,' and with a blue flash she was gone.

The Queen had summoned The Silver Fairy and Bluebell together to work out a plan of action. 'As you are now aware, Savajic the Dark Wizard, has escaped from Demodus' evil clutches but, unfortunately, he had to leave his wand behind and we know that Demodus has hidden it away somewhere in his underground kingdom. Our task is to form a plan to get it back. As we cannot enter the mines on our own without permission, it rules out using Commander Strake and her soldiers. Bluebell has come up with the idea of using Peggy Goody to lead her into the mine because she has fairy magic and can go anywhere she wishes without restriction, but if she agrees to go we will have to give her more fairy magic. Unless she can haze she would be spotted before she got within a hundred metres of the entrance. We have to decide here and now if we think she is ready for more magic and, if so, is it a wise thing for the fairy world to do?'

The Silver Fairy spoke up first. 'Peggy has shown us she has no fear with any of the tasks we have asked her to do and, equally, she has shown no fear when asked for help from her own people. She has acted without the slightest hesitation at all times, but we must also be aware that as she gets older and wiser, she will be a natural target for her government to take her into their Secret Service, and with her magic she will probably be asked to work for them out in the field as a spy. I do not have a problem with this. My only concern is for her safety, and therefore I recommend that before we make plans we should invite Peggy here and make sure she understands exactly where this magic may lead her in future.'

The Queen nodded thoughtfully. 'I completely agree,' and turning to Bluebell said, 'It's Saturday tomorrow. Do you think you can get Peggy to come here in the morning?'

'I will visit her tonight,' answered Bluebell. 'I am sure she will'.

'Then we will all meet here again tomorrow morning,' said the Queen. 'Good luck, Bluebell. Please keep me informed of your progress.'

Friday afternoon at St Ann's School was always a noisy affair with all the boys and girls restlessly waiting to get away for the weekend. Peggy and Cindy were packing away their books and discussing their plans for the next two days, but things had changed dramatically since the night of the party. As Spencer Vincent and Cindy spent more time together, Peggy hardly saw her outside of school and missed her very much. And while Cindy was with Spencer, Peggy had been spending more of her time helping her mother. The business had been thriving since Jim Smiley joined, and she was seeking planning permission to construct a purpose built laundry next to the cottage, and hopefully employ more staff. That evening while Peggy was eating her meal with her mother she told her about Cindy and Spencer, and how she missed not doing all the things together like they used to do.

'It's the way that life sometimes unfolds,' said her mother. 'When I met your father no one else seemed to exist. It was love at first sight for both of us, and we never thought we could ever love anyone else. Then you were born, and only then did we both learn that it was possible to share our love. Some day you will meet the man for you and you will know right away, and if he feels the same way then you will be so very happy. But until then you have time to do so many wonderful things, with so many bridges to cross, grasp every chance you get, and don't be in a hurry to settle down.'

That night Peggy lay in bed thinking about what her mother had said to her and about all the exiting things that could happen. 'But when would that be?' she thought. And then, suddenly, there was a bright blue flash and Bluebell was sitting at the bottom of her bed. 'Sorry if I startled you,' she said, 'but I have something very important to ask you. The Golden Fairy Queen would like you to visit her in Ireland about a matter most urgent. The Silver Fairy and I have been asked to accompany you.'

Peggy said yes without a second thought. 'I would love to. When do you want me to go?'

'Tomorrow morning,' said Bluebell. 'Can you meet me by the great oak tree at 9.30?'

'OK,' said Peggy, and before she could add another word, there was a blue flash, and Bluebell was gone.

Chapter 17

SAVAJIC'S WAND

After breakfast Peggy said goodbye to her mother and rushed to meet Bluebell at the great oak tree. 'Good morning, Peggy,' said Bluebell, floating down from a high branch. 'Good morning, Bluebell,' answered Peggy, smiling at her and holding out her hands. Bluebell held her hands and began to haze. 'First we have to meet the Silver Fairy and then we are all going to meet with the Golden Fairy Queen, so we have quite a busy day ahead of us.' And off they went.

When they arrived at the fairy site Bluebell went straight to the Silver Cave and presented Peggy to the Silver Fairy. 'Welcome, Peggy, I hope you are well. Come and sit with me. Today we are going to see our Queen. She has asked to see you about a very important matter, and so we will be going to the Golden Cave in Ireland to see her. Are you ready to go, Peggy?'

'Yes, I am,' answered Peggy. 'Good,' said the Silver Fairy, 'then please follow me.' They walked out of the Silver Cave and over to the transportation docking area. The pilot was waiting with a capsule and the top open, ready to receive her passengers. They boarded, the pilot closed the roof, and they started off. In what seemed to be a few seconds they arrived, and the pilot opened the capsule roof. They got out and walked towards the Golden Cave, and when they arrived the Queen was there, waiting to greet them.

'Your Majesty,' said the Silver Fairy. 'May I present Peggy Goody.' The Queen smiled at her. 'How good it is to see you again, Peggy. Come and sit with me. May I offer you a glass of lark's milk and honey?' 'Thank you, Your Majesty,' said Peggy, 'that would be very nice.'

Peggy settled herself and sipped her milk, and the Queen began to speak. 'On certain occasions the fairy world helps other races who need our assistance and, indeed, sometimes we in turn are helped by them. For instance, the time we helped the Leprechauns to capture Demodus and hand him over to King Igor, and the time when you helped Bluebell. Many years ago we were very fortunate to have the help of a young wizard, Savajic. He was in the forest collecting herbs and fungi for his father when he came across Fern, one of our intelligence fairies. She had been snared in a trap set by a poacher to catch birds. Savajic released her from the trap and helped her home, and so we in turn promised him help if he ever needed it. Well, he has asked us if we can help him with a certain problem, but to do it we will need your help, Peggy.'

'You have it,' said Peggy, without the slightest hesitation.

'That is very admirable of you,' replied the Queen, 'but it is not a simple task we ask of you. First, we would have to give you some extremely powerful magic, the power to haze, and before we can do that we must make sure you are aware that it takes a tremendous amount of concentration to keep it going and in turn burns up an enormous amount of energy. We can only give you the magic that enables you to haze, but the concentration and energy must come from you. We will also have to put great trust in you, because with the three magical powers you will possess, you will be superior to all other humans and you could cause untold damage if you ever so desired. The Silver Fairy and I have discussed this at great length and have concluded that we are prepared to give you that trust, but it all depends upon how you personally feel.'

Peggy looked the Queen in the eye and did not flinch. 'In the past two years I have been in danger several times and never once have I doubted that Bluebell would come to my aid. I have done impulsive things and could have hurt myself but as I get older I am getting wiser and I know that with the proper guidance I will be able to use my magical powers for both the fairy world and my own. I have already, and will continue, to trust you with my life. If you want me to help the Wizard Savajic, then I will.'

The Queen turned to the Silver Fairy. 'I have heard all the answers I need. Start training Peggy immediately and please bring her back when she can hold the haze. Only then can we proceed with a plan, and please send Bluebell to inform Savajic that Peggy has agreed to help us.'

Savajic was in his magic workshop creating a new spell. He held a heavy golden chain with a golden ball fed onto it, and the ball was inscribed with a map of the world on its surface. He had been trying to perfect his Transference Spell for weeks and now it was almost there. Suddenly, there was a blue flash and Bluebell was next to him. Savajic gave Bluebell a startled look. 'I'm sorry if I took you by surprise,' she said, 'but I can only appear in the same place as you.'

'That's alright. I'm just not used to anyone penetrating my Exclusion Spell but, of course, Bluebell, you have had my invitation.'

'The Queen has asked me to come and inform you that Peggy Goody has agreed to help us retrieve your wand from Demodus.'

'Oh, well done,' said Savajic. 'This Peggy Goody must be quite some young lady.'

'She is,' said Bluebell, 'and if anyone can get your wand back, she can. We are not sure how long it will take us because, as you well know, Demodus is a very clever and crafty creature, but as soon as I know we have it back I will let you know.' There was a blue flash and she was gone.

Commander Strake had been given the job of teaching Peggy to haze. She knew who Peggy was although she had never actually met her face to face, and Peggy would never know that she had lost two of her soldiers in a battle that had saved the lives of her mother, friends, and herself. Peggy was a good student. She was holding the haze within an hour.

'Again!' said the Commander. She would not leave anything to chance, and she knew that if the haze failed at a crucial time it meant Peggy could lose her life. She kept her going for another hour before she pronounced, 'Peggy, you can now haze.' The Commander was pleased with her work. She liked Peggy and admired the way she worked so hard, and as Peggy walked away she hoped that sometime in the future they would become good friends.

Peggy was taken back to see the Queen, and when told that Peggy could now haze she was amazed she had learned so quickly. 'Well done,' she said. 'Now, Peggy, show me.' Peggy went into a haze with such ease the Queen clapped her hands with delight. She turned to the Silver Fairy and said, 'I think it is about time we tell Peggy what this is all about.'

She looked at Peggy and said, 'We have already told you that with your help we wish to help Savajic, the Dark Wizard, but we have not told you how.

'Savajic was captured by Demodus and imprisoned in his underground kingdom, but he managed to escape. Unfortunately Demodus had taken his wand and hid it away, and when Savajic escaped he had to leave it behind. Our task is to retrieve it. The fairy world has certain ancient laws that prohibit us trespassing into other creatures' homes or property, and this is where we need your help. Humans have no such restrictions and are free to go wherever they choose. I want you to lead Bluebell down into the mines and seek out the underground kingdom of Demodus. Once there locate the wand and bring it out. We have no idea how to get into his kingdom or how far down it is, but as you search Bluebell will be mapping out the way you take so you can find your way back, and Hawk Eye in your helmets will record everything you see. Then we will have a plan of his tunnels.

'I do not need to tell you how dangerous this mission will be and the consequences you face if you are caught, but with the magic you both possess you should be more than a match for Demodus and his Demodoms.'

'I understand,' said Peggy, 'and I'm not afraid with Bluebell at my side, but may I ask you a question, Your Majesty?'

'Yes, of course you can. What is it you wish to know?'

'Well,' said Peggy thoughtfully, 'if Savajic is a Dark Wizard why do we want to help him? And wouldn't it be better to leave his wand so he couldn't use it for evil?'

The Queen smiled at Peggy. 'The title Dark Wizard is an unfortunate name given to students who have graduated from The Black Eagle School for Wizards. It has nothing to do with wicked deeds. There are two schools, the other being the White, and so the term Dark just signifies to you which school they graduated from. But a very good question. Now, Peggy, I would like you to go home and get a good night's sleep, and in the morning have a big breakfast because you will need every single ounce of energy you can hold. We go at 10.00 am tomorrow. Bluebell will meet you by the great oak tree at 9.30. I will say goodbye until then.'

The Silver Fairy said goodbye to the Queen and went with Peggy and Bluebell to the transportation docking area where they boarded the capsule and travelled back to the Silver Cave. Bluebell escorted Peggy back to the great oak tree, and this time she was hazing by herself. 'I will meet you here in the morning,' said Bluebell, and she was gone.

The next morning, while Peggy was having breakfast with her mother, she told her she was going to visit Bluebell, but no more than that, otherwise she might start to worry. She finished eating and helped her mother wash the dishes and clear away. Peggy tried to act as casually as possible and not show how anxious she really was. She put on her coat and said she would probably be out all day. 'You just be careful what you are doing in that forest, young lady, and don't be too late,' said her mother.

Peggy wasted no time getting down to the great oak tree and when she arrived Bluebell was waiting there. They exchanged greetings and started off for the Silver Cave. Peggy slipped into a haze as if it was second nature and Bluebell smiled but said nothing. It was just what she wanted to see. When they arrived Bluebell took Peggy straight to the transport docking area where a capsule was waiting for them. The Silver Fairy had already left for the Golden Cave and would now be with the Queen going over their plan.

As soon as they arrived they headed for the Golden Cave. The Queen invited them in and they began to study the plan. There was not much to it really: after they entered the mine it would all be new territory, but a reconnaissance had pin pointed where Demodus posted his guards and it also highlighted five separate trip wires that would give away any unexpected visitors. They were placed in such a way that to avoid them the only way into the camp and the mine entrance was a heavily guarded narrow pathway, and that was just their first hurdle. Without the ability to haze it would have been impossible for Peggy to get past the guards.

The Queen turned to Peggy and asked if she was ready to go. 'Yes,' said Peggy confidently, but in truth her stomach was churning. The Queen raised her hands as if in blessing, 'Good, then may good fortune go with you. And remember that the moment you enter the mines you will both be on your own, so stay alert and at no time drop your guard.'

Bluebell led Peggy past the first guard. It would tell them whether the Demodoms could pick up Peggy's scent. He did not even flinch, and it was a good sign. They had passed six guards and were approaching the narrow path that led directly to the camp, and at the end were two Demodoms. 'If only Peggy could fly,' thought Bluebell, 'it would make this so much easier.' She would somehow need to distract the guards so Peggy could slip past them unnoticed. She whispered to her, 'Get up close, then stand still. I am going to fly over them and attract their attention. As soon as they turn around be ready to make a dash through the gap because you will not get a second chance.'

Bluebell took off into the air and landed behind the guards. She picked up a small stone and froze. Coming up behind Peggy was a Demodom guard. She hurled the stone at one of the guards and hit him in the middle of the back. He yelled out, 'What was that?' and as they both turned around to look, Peggy took off like a sprinter from out of the blocks. She got level with Bluebell and they both looked at each other and sighed with relief. Peggy was wearing trainers and Bluebell noticed that as she walked she was leaving a footprint in the dust. 'Stop!' she cried, and pointed down to her foot prints. 'Walk on your tip toes. That way you will blend in with the Demodoms' paw prints.'

Peggy went immediately up onto her toes. 'We are nearly there,' whispered Bluebell. 'Let's hope no one notices and raises the alarm.' Then, at last, they were past the guards, through the entrance and into the cave. It was larger than they had expected, which suited Peggy, because it meant she could walk upright. She had never seen Demodus and guessed he must be taller than his Demodoms. They walked for about two hundred metres before they came across many more Demodoms in a large cave, and it looked like most of them were sleeping. At the far end of the cave were two more tunnels. They crept carefully over towards them and, when they got there, found they were both identical. 'Which one do we take?' asked Peggy.

'Unfortunately, only one at a time,' said Bluebell. 'Let's start with this one. We may be lucky.' As they entered they were surprised to find how well lit it was. All the lighting was modern and the tunnel seemed to come alive. Deeper and deeper they went until they reached another cave, and when they entered their blood ran cold. Inside was a massive laboratory, where there were several humans, men in white coats, all working computers. It looked like they were growing creatures in glass cubicles.

'Get in closer,' whispered Bluebell, 'and let's get a better look.' And just as they moved into the cave they could hear heavy foot steps coming up fast behind them. It was Demodus. 'How many more have you got ready?' he growled at the men in white coats. Peggy had to stop herself from crying out. She had never seen anything so frightening and so ugly before. Bluebell grabbed her arm. 'Don't move,' she whispered.

Demodus walked over to the men. 'Well!' he grunted. One of the men said; there are twenty-five more ready to come out now. We have just finished stabilising their breathing.' Suddenly there was a clicking noise and twenty-five of the doors sprang open, and as the mist inside the cubicles cleared they could see twenty-five Demodoms. But these were different. Instead of the normal sharp claws, they had grown normal hands and their shoulders were wider.

'Excellent!' said Demodus. 'When will they be ready for weapons training?'

'Just as soon as we have completed all the checks on them, I would say in about an hour.'

'And how are the others?' he demanded.

'They are on the shooting range,' answered the man.

Demodus turned and went toward a tunnel that ran off from the other side of the cave. 'Follow him,' said Bluebell. 'We must not let him out of our sight.' They travelled seven hundred metres down another brightly lit tunnel and all the time Bluebell was recording direction and distance. She would know exactly where they were at all times.

Up ahead they could hear what sounded like gunfire and as it got louder they entered another massive cave that must have been at least one thousand metres in length and had been made into an army-type shooting range with rows of sand bags every hundred metres. Peggy counted forty Demodoms all taking shooting lessons, and again there were several humans this time, dressed in army uniforms and shouting out instructions. Demodus was building himself an army, and this time they would be able to handle weapons.

Demodus watched with great interest at the progress of his new breed of Demodoms. He suddenly let out a spine chilling laugh. He roared, 'This will show you fairies not to meddle in my affairs! Let's see how you get on against my armour—piercing bullets.'

Peggy looked at Bluebell. She was understandably very worried. 'Shall we go back and tell the Queen?'

'No,' said Bluebell. 'We have a mission to complete. We must retrieve Savajic's wand.'

After what seemed to be an eternity for Peggy, Demodus was on the move again, thundering back up the tunnel toward the laboratory. They followed closely on his heels, desperate not to lose sight of him. As he entered the laboratory he stopped and growled, 'Make sure they get sent for weapons training!' and then he headed back up towards the cave where his Demodoms were sleeping. As he entered several of them fell to their knees and Demodus walked past, ignoring them. He turned into the twin tunnel and started walking down, grunting to himself as he went. It was perfect because the more noise he made the less chance they had of being detected. They followed him closely for eight hundred metres, and walked into a magnificent cave. It was a different shape to all the others. It had been mined out of solid rock to resemble the rooms of an English stately home, and all of the treasures Demodus had stolen from his raids on grand houses were displayed to perfection. It was truly splendid.

He made his way to the dining room, where a meal had been laid out for him. Ten years ago he had tunnelled his way under a famous restaurant in London where the staff slept on the premises at night. He had captured one of the chefs and the head waiter, imprisoned them, and made them prepare and serve all his meals and run his home. All this had been a complete secret known only to him, until now.

Bluebell whispered to Peggy, 'We wait now and hope that Demodus leads us to the wand.' As he ate he grunted, and because of his claws he was unable to hold a knife and fork easily, so he picked up the plate and tipped it into his wide ugly mouth, chewed it up, and swallowed it down. The food looked wonderful but it was doubtful he even tasted it. After he had consumed several plates of various courses and several bottles of wine, he sat back and growled, 'That's better,' and got up. He crossed the room and went into what looked like a large study, but before they could follow him in he closed the door behind him.

'This could be difficult,' said Bluebell. 'We can't get in from the outside because there isn't one. Have you got any ideas, Peggy?'

'We could wait and perhaps he might fall asleep. Then we can get in and close the door behind us.' But just as she finished speaking the man who had been serving table came carrying a silver tray with a decanter of brandy and a large glass. 'Here's our chance!' said Bluebell. The man knocked on the door and Demodus growled 'Come in,' and as he opened the door and went in they followed closely behind. The room was surrounded by bookshelves filled with leather bound volumes stolen from famous collections across the country. He was seated behind an ornately carved desk, and as Peggy looked, her heart skipped a beat. Lying on top of the desk, in front of him, was Savajic's wand. She pointed to it and Bluebell nodded. They were standing motionless, hoping Demodus would drink his brandy and fall asleep. The man put the tray down and left the room, carefully closing the door behind him.

Demodus sat mumbling to himself and staring at the wand. 'What secrets do you hold and how do I release them?' He picked it up and slowly twirled it between his wicked looking claws. The drink was beginning to take effect. Then, suddenly, he looked directly at Peggy and sniffed the air. His cavernous nostrils, opening and closing, taking in a scent he vaguely recognised. 'No,' he mumbled, 'not in here, not possible, not possible.' His head dropped down onto his chest and he was asleep.

Bluebell looked over at Peggy. 'Are you alright?' she asked.

'Yes, I'm OK, but I really thought he had picked up my scent.'

'He probably did, but fortunately for us he was too drunk for it to register with him. Give him five more minutes, to make sure he's fast asleep, then we make our move.'

While they waited Bluebell told Peggy to pan one side of the study while she panned the other. As Peggy slowly looked around, recording every detail, she saw a beautiful sword hanging on the wall behind Demodus. 'I suppose he stole that from someone's treasured collection,' she told herself. Peggy crept closer to the desk. Demodus had let the wand fall from his claws. All she had to do was pick it up and it would disappear from view. She stretched over the desk towards the wand and as she picked it up Demodus opened his eyes and the wand disappeared in front of him as if by magic.

'Goody!' he roared, and slashed at the air in front of him. 'I knew it! I could smell you.' He stood up in a rage, slashing at the air with his evil claws. Peggy picked up a heavy leather chair and sent it crashing into his chest, knocking him backwards and onto the floor. 'Follow me,' said Bluebell. She opened the door and they ran through, slamming it behind them. Demodus pushed the chair off him and staggered to his feet. He could not understand how she had got into his home undetected. What had she seen? How much did she know? She must be stopped at all costs!

He had installed speakers in all the caves and picked up the hand set. 'There are intruders in the caves! Block all entrances immediately!' The Demodoms leapt into action. They could not see any intruders but started to block all the entrances. Bluebell was at full speed with Peggy close behind. They had already passed through the cave where most of the Demodoms were and headed toward the entrance. They had ten metres to go when Peggy suddenly fell. She had tripped over a rock that had fallen and been left there, and as she got up a large stone was rolled across the entrance of the cave. She was trapped and Bluebell was outside.

Now she would be tested to her limit. As she tried to stand up she could hear Demodus screaming 'Stop them, stop them!' Peggy wedged herself against the rock wall of the cave and put both feet on the stone. She closed her eyes and said 'UP-UP.' Slowly her legs got longer and longer and the stone began to move, then a gap appeared, but she could hear Demodus getting closer, and her energy level was dropping. She could feel it. She had been hazing for almost three hours. 'One more push,' she told herself, and as the stone toppled over she screamed 'DOWN-DOWN.' She was back on her feet and running now. Nothing was going to stop her. As she approached the path that lead away from the mine she could see that five Demodoms were blocking it. She ran directly at them, smashing into them and sending them in all directions. She did not stop until she was in the forest.

'What happened?' said a voice. It was Bluebell, sitting in a tree above her.

'Would you believe that I tripped over a rock right by the end of the tunnel?' Bluebell said, 'I'm beginning to believe anything about you, Peggy' and they both burst out laughing.

The Queen was delighted when Bluebell sent her news that they had been successful in their mission and on their way back. The whole operation had only taken a little over three hours, although it seemed more like three days to Peggy.

When the capsule arrived at the Golden Cave, there were crowds of fairies cheering them. Peggy felt embarrassed, but

Bluebell leaned over to her and said, 'This is something you are going to have to get used to.'

The Queen and The Silver Fairy were waiting for them at the Golden Cave. 'Congratulations, Peggy,' said the Queen. Peggy thanked the Queen and handed her Savajic's wand. The Queen held up her hand. Thank you Peggy but I have a better idea. I would like you to meet Savajic Menglor.'

She turned and looked at him. He was nothing like she had pictured him. There was no pointed hat and long flowing cloak, as she thought all wizards wore. Instead there was a tall slim, good looking man, immaculately dressed in a pin stripe suit, white shirt with tie to match, and black brogue shoes. His hair was shoulder length, wavy and brushed back.

'I thought you would like to give it back in person,' said the Queen, smiling at her. Peggy hesitated for a moment and then handed him the wand.

'I believe that this is yours, Mr Menglor. Please accept it as a favour from the Queen.'

Savajic bowed towards the Queen, then turned to Peggy and bowed again. 'I accept it with enormous respect and gratitude to the fairy world and to you, Peggy, a worthy ally.'

Meanwhile Bluebell had gone directly to be debriefed and transfer the information from her helmet into the hologram system, and when it had been completed she went back to inform the Queen. Savajic had taken Peggy to one side while Bluebell was talking to the Queen. He was asking her about her family and friends and her school. She told him she had lost her father when she was just a baby and how much she loved her mother. They talked about all kinds of things and felt easy with each other and then the Queen interrupted their conversation and invited both of them to the hologram room. She turned to Savajic, 'I would like you to see this. It is most worrying.'

They sat down and the hologram system started. It showed exactly what Bluebell had seen from start to finish. They played the laboratory and the firing range sequences several times over, making comments as it played.

After it was finished the Queen was visibly shocked and concerned. 'You must realise that from now on we will be facing a murderous army fully trained and armed with the most sophisticated of human weapons.' She gestured to Savajic, 'Losing your wand has done us a massive service. I thank you.'

Savajic smiled at Peggy. 'Your Majesty, I think our gratitude should be directed to Peggy. Without her help and her courage none of this would have been unearthed and we would both have been none the wiser to this new deadly threat that Demodus poses.'

The fairy in charge of the hologram coughed. 'Your Majesty, the programme from Peggy's helmet is ready for viewing.' They turned and began to watch. It was very much the same until she entered the study of Demodus, and as she looked around Savajic suddenly shouted 'Stop!'

The hologram came to a sudden halt. Peggy was looking at the sword on the wall. Savajic had gone quite pale and looked like a ghost and for a moment was speechless. As he regained his composure he asked if the fairy could zoom into the picture of the sword so he could read the words on the blade. As the sword got larger the words became clear.

Savajic said in total disbelief, 'It's The Sword of Destiny. How could he possibly have got his hands on it?' He turned to the Queen. 'Your Majesty, we are in more danger than you could possibly imagine. The Sword of Destiny was responsible for the bloodiest war the Wizard World has ever known. Baldric Zealotte was a powerful wizard and totally power crazy. He made a pact with Kanzil, The Lord of the Magma, that in exchange for his soul he would make him a sword that could overcome and kill anything on earth. It was fashioned in the furnaces of hell, and nothing could withstand its awesome power.

'Baldric Zealotte's followers, a band of powerful and evil wizards who were called the Death Riders, waged war against the Wizard World, showing no mercy, killing wizards, women, and children alike. The war lasted for three whole years, until Goodrick the Elder, leader of the Council of Wizards, trapped Zealotte in a time warp bubble and sent him spinning into space to be lost forever. The Sword of Destiny was hidden by Goodrick, a secret he took with him to the grave.

'The legend of the Sword has lived on for over a thousand years, and there have been stories of sightings, but all have been proved untrue. I believe Demodus is not aware of its powers, but if he ever finds out, our worlds will be in terrible peril. We are all aware of his murderous ways. Somehow we have to stop him from finding out. I will have to inform the Council of Wizards immediately.'

The Queen said, 'I truly believe that somewhere it is written that destiny ordained our paths to meet out in the forest, and join our three races together in an unbreakable triangle of Fairy, Human and Wizard. A triangle forged out of honesty and decency, to fight against evil. None of us sought it, it was fate. My only concern is that Peggy is still only a young girl of fourteen and although we have given her very powerful magic, she is still very vulnerable to many things. For instance, Demodus picked up

Peggy's scent and could have captured her, but we can't change that.'

'I can,' said Savajic.

'Well,' said the Queen, 'we had to walk Peggy through a mine field of Demodoms because she can't fly, and we can't make her fly.'

'I can,' said Savajic.

'You can fly?' asked the Queen.

'Better than that,' said Savajic, 'I can transport myself to any point on earth in an instant, and I could do the same for Peggy and teach her many more spells.'

Savajic looked at Peggy. 'Would you like me to teach you?'

Peggy looked to the Queen for guidance. 'You certainly have my blessing, Peggy said the Queen.

'Yes, please, Mr Menglor,' answered Peggy.

'Call me Savajic, please. We are friends, are we not?'

Peggy laughed out loud, but it was a nervous laugh, and they all realised how tired she must be feeling. Savajic kissed Peggy on the hand and said he would be contacting her shortly. He said goodbye to the Queen and made his exit. The Queen thanked Peggy once again and asked Bluebell to see her home safely.

When Peggy arrived home her mother was preparing the evening meal. 'That's good timing,' she said, 'have you had a nice day?'

'Yes, thank you, mother, quiet but nice. Have I got time for a bath before dinner? Yes, I'll be another thirty minutes or so.'

Peggy filled the bath and used her best bath lotion. She slowly sank down into the bath and closed her eye's, it was so warm and peaceful. She wondered what Savajic was going to teach her, and would she ever be clever enough to learn different spells. A hundred questions spun around in her head. Her eyes were closed but she could see The Sword of Destiny hanging on the wall in Demodus' study.

She sighed out loud, and then concentrated on the meal her mother was cooking downstairs. 'I'm starving,' she said to herself.

The End